THUNDER ON THE LEFT

by

CHRISTOPHER MORLEY

FIRST PUBLISHED MARCH, 1926
NEW IMPRESSIONS APRIL, MAY, JUNE, 1926
CHEAP EDITION (3/6), 1927
FIRST ISSUED IN THE TRAVELLERS' LIBRARY 1928
NEW IMPRESSION JANUARY, 1929

ISBN 978-1-4067-9489-2

TO
S. A. E.

PREFACE

I AM aware of a certain hesitation in writing this pre-
face to Mr. Morley's book ; I seem to have involved
myself rather arrogantly during the last year or two in
the prefacing of American works of fiction. You may
well ask what business is it of mine, why don't I let them
speak for themselves ? But I think the explanation lies
in this, that a number of us who are keenly interested
in the modern American novel feel that there is just now
in England a conviction far too widely spread that the
American novel of to-day is following always a convention, a convention either of the Middle West and the
small American town, or of the cow-boy and the rescued
heroine, or of the smart night life of New York. Of
course there is no truth in this whatever, the new
American novel is rapidly becoming one of the most
individual forces in the world of literature. We have
only to consider that during the last few years we have
had Cabell's *Jurgen*, Sinclair Lewis' *Babbitt*, Willa
Cather's *Lost Lady*, Carl van Vechten's *Peter Whiffle*,
Scott Fitzgerald's *The Great Gatsby*, to realise the thrilling differences of the new American fiction.

And now Christopher Morley's *Thunder on the Left*
surely joins this list. Whatever else you may say about
the book this at least is true, that nobody else in the wide
world could have written it, and that was at one time
the last thing I would have expected ever to say about
this writer's work. For, delightful though his earlier

essays, phantasies and poetry have been, they were of a
recognised fantastic sentimental school and the dangerous name of Barrie seemed to have been written over
Mr. Morley's private door. Barrie's perilous moments
(and there have been many) have been saved, often
when one thought that all was lost, by rescues of genius,
but that has made his school a dangerous one to work in.
As with Barrie's own sometimes irritating infant there
has seemed a danger that Christopher Morley was never
going to grow up, and then suddenly, without a word of
warning, he produces this astonishingly mature work.
His gifts were as many as they were dangerous and that
especial danger of finding life too enchanting to be true
is difficult to escape because it becomes so easily a habit ;
but in *Thunder on the Left* the beauty and the fantasy are
present as emphatically as ever they have been in Mr.
Morley's work, but to them many other things are added.
You may say if you like to be very self-confident that
you don't know what this book means (there will be
people who will say this) or you may interpret it at its
simplest (if you do this you will be laughed at by clever
people who see in it much more than you do) or you
may be wonderfully subtle about it and use it as a pro-
vocative of your own brilliance (and then people will
say how conceited you have become), and this is I think
one of the greatest powers of the book, that it is personal
to every reader, it will become for everyone a reflection
of himself. I don't wish this to sound too alarming.
At its simplest it is a story of certain children who,
feeling the difference between their own world and that
of their elders, thought that they would be spies and
discover this country into which they must themselves

The undertaking a comedy not merely sentimental was very dangerous.

—OLIVER GOLDSMITH.

On parla des passions. "Ah! qu'elles sont funestes!" disait Zadig.—"Ce sont les vents qui enflent les voiles du vaisseau," repartit l'ermite: "elles le submergent quelquefois; mais sans elles il ne pourrait voguer. La bile rend colère et malade; mais sans la bile l'homme ne saurait vivre. Tout est dangereux ici-bas, et tout est nécessaire."

—VOLTAIRE, *Zadig.*

"Your mind had to be tormented and fevered and exalted before you could see a god."

"It was cruel of you to do this," she said.

—JAMES STEPHENS,
In the Land of Youth.

THUNDER ON THE LEFT

Thunder on the Left

I

NOW that the children were getting big, it wasn't to be called the Nursery any longer. In fact, it was being repapered that very day: the old scribbled Mother Goose pattern had already been covered with new strips, damp and bitter-smelling. But Martin thought he would be able to remember the gay fairy-tale figures, even under the bright fresh paper. There were three bobtailed mice, dancing. They were repeated several times in the procession of pictures that ran round the wall. How often he had studied them as he lay in bed waiting for it to be time to get up. It must be excellent to be Grown Up and able to dress as early as you please. What a golden light lies across the garden those summer mornings.

At any rate, it would be comforting to know that the bobtailed mice were still there, underneath. To-day the smell of the paste and new

paper was all through the house. The men were
to have come last week. To-day it was awkward:
it was Martin's birthday (he was ten) and he and
Bunny had been told to invite some friends for a
small party. It was raining, too: one of those
steady drumming rains that make a house so cosy.
The Grown Ups were having tea on the veranda,
so the party was in the dining room. When Mrs.
Richmond looked through the glass porch doors
to see how they were getting on, she was surprised
to find no one visible.

"Where on earth have those children gone?"
she exclaimed. "How delightfully quiet they are."

There was a seven-voiced halloo of triumph,
and a great scuffle and movement under the big
mahogany table. Several steamer rugs had been
pinned together and draped across the board so
that they hung down forming a kind of pavilion.
From this concealment the children came scrambling and surrounded her in a lively group.

"We had all disappeared!" said Bunny. She was
really called Eileen, but she was soft and plump
and brown-eyed and twitch-nosed; three years
younger than her brother.

"You came just in time to save us," said Martin
gaily.

"Just in time to save my table," amended Mrs.

Richmond. "Bunny, you know how you cried when you scratched your legs going blackberrying. Do you suppose the table likes having its legs scratched any better than you do? And those grimy old rugs all over my lace cloth. Martin, take them off at once."

"We were playing Stern Parents," explained Alec, a cousin and less awed by reproof than the other guests, who were merely friends.

Mrs. Richmond was taken aback. "What a queer name for a game."

"It's a lovely game," said Ruth, her face pink with excitement. "You pretend to be Parents and you all get together and talk about the terrible time you have with your children——"

Martin broke in: "And you tell each other all the things you've had to scold them for——"

"And you have to forbid their doing all kinds of things," said Ben.

"And speak to them Very Seriously," chirped Bunny. Mrs. Richmond felt a twinge of merriment at the echo of this familiar phrase.

"And every time you've punished them for something that doesn't really matter——" (this was Phyllis)

"——You're a *Stern Parent*, and have to disappear!" cried Martin.

"You get under the table and can't come out until someone says something nice about you."

"It's a very instructing game, 'cause you have to know just how far children can be allowed to go——"

"But we were *all* Stern Parents, and had all disappeared."

"Yes, and then Mother said we were delightfully quiet, and that saved us."

"What an extraordinary game," said Mrs. Richmond.

"All Martin's games are extraordinary," said Phyllis. "He just made up one called Quarrelsome Children."

"Will you play it with us?" asked Bunny.

"I don't believe that's a new game," said her mother. "I'm sure I've seen it played, too often. But it's time for the cake. Straighten up the chairs and I'll go and get it."

Seated round the table, and left alone with the cake, the lighted candles, and the ice cream, the children found much to discuss.

"Ten candles," said Alec, counting them carefully.

"I had thirteen on mine, last birthday," said Phyllis, the oldest of the girls.

"That's nothing, so did I," said Ben.

"Your cook's clever," said Ruth. "She's marked the places to cut, with icing, so you can make all the pieces even."

"I think it was foolish of her," said Martin, "because Bunny is quite a small child still; if she has too much chocolate she comes out in spots."

Bunny and Joyce, at the other end of the table, looked at each other fleetingly, in a tacit alliance of juniority. Joyce was also seven, a dark little elf, rather silent.

"Why don't you blow out the candles?" shrilled Bunny.

This effectively altered the topic. After the sudden hurricane had ceased, Martin began to cut, obediently following the white spokes of sugar.

"I wonder what it feels like to be grown up?" said Alec.

"I guess we'll know if we wait long enough," said Phyllis.

"How old do you have to be, to be grown up?" asked Ruth.

"A man's grown up when he's twenty-one," Ben stated firmly.

"Is Daddy twenty-one?" said Bunny.

Cries of scorn answered this. "Of course he is," said Martin. "Daddy's middle-age, he's over thirty. He's what they call *primeoflife*, I heard him say so."

"That's just before your hair begins to come out in the comb," said Alec.

Bunny was undismayed, perhaps encouraged by seeing in front of her more ice cream than she had ever been left alone with before.

"Daddy *isn't* grown up," she insisted. "The other day when we played blind man's buff on the beach, Mother said he was just a big boy."

"Girls grow up quicker," said Phyllis. "My sister's eighteen, she's so grown up she'll hardly speak to me. It happened all at once. She went for a week-end party, when she came back she was grown up."

"That's not grown up," said Ben. "That's just stuck up. Girls get like that. It's a form of nervousness."

They were not aware that Ben had picked up this phrase by overhearing it applied to some eccentricities of his own. They were impressed, and for a moment the ice cream and cake engaged all attentions. Then a round of laughter from the veranda reopened the topic.

"Why do men laugh more than ladies?" asked Bunny.

"It must be wonderful," said Martin.

"You bet!" said Ben. "Think of having long trousers, and smoking a pipe, blowing rings, going to town every day, going to the bank and getting money——"

"And all the drug stores where you can stop and have sodas," said Ruth.

"Sailing a boat!"

"Going shopping!"

"The circus!" shouted Bunny.

"I don't mean just *doing* things," said Martin. "I mean thinking things." His eager face, clearly lit by two candles in tall silver sticks, was suddenly and charmingly grave. "Able to think what you want to; not to have to—to do things you know are wrong." For an instant the boy seemed to tremble on the edge of uttering the whole secret infamy of childhood; the most pitiable of earth's slaveries; perhaps the only one that can never be dissolved. But the others hardly understood; nor did he, himself. He covered his embarrassment by grabbing at a cracker of gilt paper in which Alec was rummaging for the pull.

Joyce had slipped from her chair and was peeping through one of the windows. Something in the talk had struck home to her in a queer, troublesome way. Suddenly, she didn't know why, she wanted to look at the Grown Ups, to see exactly what they were like. The rest of the party followed her in a common impulse. Joyce's attitude caused them to tiptoe across the room and peer covertly from behind the long curtains. Without a word of explanation all were aware of their odd feeling of spying on the enemy—an implacable enemy, yet one who is (how plainly we realize it when we see him off guard in the opposing trench, busy at his poor affairs, cooking or washing his socks) so kin to ourselves. With the apprehensive alertness of those whose lives may depend on their nimble observation, they watched the unconscious group at the tea table.

"Daddy's taking three lumps," said Bunny. She spoke louder than is prudent in an outpost, and was s-s-sh-ed.

"Your mother's got her elbow on the table," Ruth whispered.

"Daddy's smacking his lips and chomping," insisted Bunny.

"That's worse than talking with your mouth full."

"How queer they look when they laugh."

"Your mother lifts her head like a hen swallowing."

"Yours has her legs crossed."

"It's a form of nervousness."

"They do all the things they tell us not to," said Joyce.

"Look, he's reaching right across the table for another cake."

Martin watched his parents and their friends. What was there in the familiar scene that became strangely perplexing? He could not have put it into words, but there was something in those voices and faces that made him feel frightened, a little lonely. Was that really Mother, by the silver urn with the blue flame flattened under it? He could tell by her expression that she was talking about things that belong to that Other World, the thrillingly exciting world of Parents, whose secrets are so cunningly guarded. That world changes the subject, alters the very tone of its voice, when you approach. He had a wish to run out on the veranda, to reassure himself by the touch of her soft cool arm in the muslin dress. He wanted to touch the teapot, to see if it was hot. If it was, he would know that all this was real. They had gone so far away.—Or were they also only playing a game?

"They look as though they were hiding something," he said.

"They're having fun," Phyllis said. "They always do; grown ups have a wonderful time."

"Come on,"—Martin remembered that he was the host—"the ice cream will get cold." This was what Daddy always said.

Bunny felt a renewed pride as she climbed into her place at the end of the table. Martin looked solemnly handsome in his Eton collar across the shining spread of candlelight and cloth and pink peppermints. The tinted glass panes above the sideboard were cheerful squares of colour against the wet grey afternoon. She wriggled a little, to reëstablish herself on the slippery chair.

"Our family is getting very grown up," she said happily. "We're not going to have a nursery any more. It's going to be the guest room."

"I don't think I want to be grown up," said Alec suddenly. "It's silly. I don't believe they have a good time at all.'

This was a disconcerting opinion. Alec, as an older cousin, held a position of some prestige. A faint dismay was apparent in the gazes that crossed rapidly in the sparkling waxlight.

"I think we ought to make up our minds about it," Martin said gravely. "Pretty soon, the way things are going, we *will* be, then it'll be too late."

"Silly, what can you do?" said Phyllis. "Of course we've got to grow up, everyone does, unless they die." Her tone was clear and positive, but also there was a just discernible accent of inquiry. She had not yet quite lost her childhood birthright of wonder, of belief that almost anything is possible.

"We'd have to Take Steps," cried Alec, unconsciously quoting the enemy. "We could just decide among ourselves that we simply wouldn't, and if we all lived together we could go on just like we are."

"It would be like a game," said Martin, glowing.

"With toys?" ejaculated Bunny, entranced.

Ben was firmly opposed. "I won't do it. I want to have long trousers and grow a moustache."

Martin's face was serious with the vision of huge alternatives.

"That's it," he said. "We've got to know before we can decide. It's terribly important. If they *don't* have a good time, we'd better——"

"We could *ask* them if they're happy," exclaimed Ruth, thrilled by the thought of running out on the veranda to propose this stunning question.

"They wouldn't tell you," said Alec. "They're too polite."

Phyllis was trying to remember instructive examples of adult infelicity. "They don't tell the truth," she agreed. "Mother once said that if

Daddy went on like that she'd go mad, and I waited and waited, and he did and she didn't."

"You mustn't believe what they say," Martin continued. "They never tell the truth if they think children are around. They don't *want* us to know what it's like."

"Perhaps they're ashamed of being grown up," Ben suggested.

"We must find out," Martin said, suddenly feeling in his mind the expanding brightness of an idea. "It'll be a new game. We'll all be spies in the enemy's country, we'll watch them and see exactly how they behave, and bring in a report."

"Get hold of their secret codes, and find where their forces are hidden," cried Ben, who liked the military flavour of this thought.

"I think it's a silly game," said Phyllis. "You can't really find out anything; and if you did, you'd be punished. Spies always get caught."

"Penalty of death!" shouted the boys, elated.

"It's harder than being a real spy," said Martin. "You can't wear the enemy's uniform and talk their language. But I'm going to do it, anyhow."

"Me too!" Joyce exclaimed from the other end of the table, where she and Bunny had followed the conversation with half-frightened excitement.

"I want to be a spy!" added Bunny.

"Mustn't have too many spies," said Alec. "The enemy would suspect something was up. Send one first, he'll see what he can find and report to us."

It was not clear to Bunny exactly who the enemy were or how the spying was to be carried out; but if Martin was to do it, it would be well done, she was certain. Spying, that suggested secrecy, and secrecy——

"Martin has a little roll-top desk with a key!" she shouted. "Daddy gave it to him for his birthday."

"Oh, I forgot," said Phyllis. She ran out into the living room, and returned with a large parcel. "Many happy returns," she said, laying it in front of Martin. If you listen intently, behind the innocent little phrase you can overhear, like a whispering chorus, the voices of innumerable parents: "And don't forget, when you give it to him, to say *Many happy returns.*"

The others also hurried to get the packages that had been left in the vestibule. There was a great rattling of paper and untying of string; an embarrassed reiteration of thankyous by Martin. He felt it awkward to say the same thing again for each gift.

Hearing the movement in the dining room, the grown ups had now come in.

"Such a pretty sight."

"I love children's parties, their faces are always a picture."

"Martin, did you say thankyou to Alec for that lovely croquet set?"

"This is what *I* gave him," said Ben, pushing forward the parcheesi board.

"The girls are so dainty, like little flowers."

"Who is the little dark one, over by the window?"

"That's Joyce.—Why, Joyce dear, what are you crying about?"

The strong maternal voice rang through the room with a terrible publicity of compassion. The children stared. Bunny ran and threw her arms round her friend, who had hidden her face in the curtain. Bunny thought she knew what was wrong. Joyce had forgotten to bring a present, and was ashamed because all the others had done so. The miserable little figure tried to efface itself in the curtain; even the tiny pearl buttons at the back of her pink frock had come undone. Things that are close to us, how loyal they are, how they follow the moods of their owners.

"There, there, honey, what's the trouble? After such a lovely party?" This was authoritative pity, threateningly musical.

Bunny pressed her warm lips against a wet petal of nostril.

"Martin doesn't mind," she whispered. "He *hates* presents."

Joyce could feel powerful fingers buttoning the cool gap between her shoulders. When that was done she would be turned round and asked what was the matter.

"Perhaps she has a pain," boomed a masculine vibration. "These parties always upset them. Worst thing for children."

Joyce could smell a whiff of cigar and see large feet in white canvas shoes approaching. Best to face it now before worse happens. She turned desperately, hampered by Bunny's embrace, almost throttling her in an excess of affection. Breaking away she ran across the room, where Martin and the boys were averting their eyes from the humiliation of the would-be spy. She thrust into his hand a tiny package, damp now.

"It was so small," she said.

A moment of appalling silence hung over the trembling pair. Martin could feel it coming, the words "What do you say, Martin?" seemed forming and rolling up over his head like opal banks of summer storm. Yet he could not have said a word. He seized her hand and shook it, with a grotesque bob of his head.

"Such a little gentleman, how *do* you train them? I can't do anything with Ben, he's so rough."

Joyce was blotted out by a merciful hooded raincoat. As she struggled through its dark rubber-smelling folds she could hear voices coming down from above.

"Alec, say good-bye to your little cousins— no, we must say your *big* cousins, mustn't we?"

"Thank Mrs. Richmond for such a nice party."

"Thank you, Mrs. Richmond, for such a nice party."

"Martin, you haven't opened Joyce's present."

"I don't want to open it," murmured Martin sullenly. Then he knew he had said the wrong thing.

"Don't want to open it? Why of course you want to open it. We don't measure presents by their size, do we, Joyce?"

Joyce, almost escaped, was drawn again into the arena.

"Come, Alec, we'll see what Joyce has given Martin and then you must go."

"I can't untie it, the string's wet," muttered Martin.

The watching circle drew closer.

"Wet? Nonsense. Here, give it to me."

Unfolding of sodden paper. A mouse of soft grey plush, with little glassy eyes and a long silky tail. And two wheels under his stomach, a key to wind him by.

"Why, it's the mouse we saw in the window at the cigar store. Joyce was crazy about it."

"You see, Martin, she's given you a mouse because she wanted it so much for herself."

"It isn't very much, my dear, but there's so little to choose from, here in the country."

"It's like the mice we had on the nursery wall-paper," said Bunny, praising valiantly.

"Wind it up and see it run."

There are some situations that, once entered, must be carried through to the end. Martin wound. He could tell by the feel of the key that something was wrong.

"I'll play with it later," he said.

"Don't be so stubborn, Martin. We're all waiting to see it."

Joyce's gaze was riveted on the mouse. She remembered the ominous click in its vitals, when she had been giving it an ecstatic trial. But perhaps Martin, with the magic boys have in these matters, could make it go again, as it went—so thrillingly, in mouselike darts and curves—on the cigar-store floor.

Martin put it down, giving it a deft push. It ran a few inches and stopped.

"It runs fine," he said hastily. "But it won't go here on the rug."

"Let's see it," said Ben, whose mechanical sense was not satisfied by so brief an exhibition.

"It's mine," snapped Martin fiercely, and put it in his pocket.

"We really must go," said someone.

"Would you each like a piece of Martin's cake to take home?"

"Oh, no, thank you, I think they've had plenty."

"Did you make a wish?"

"No, we forgot," said Martin.

"Oh, what a pity. When you blow out the candles on a birthday cake you should always make a wish."

"Will it come true?"

"If it's a nice wish."

"Light them again and do it now," said one of the parents. The drill must be finished.

"Yes, do, before the children go."

"Will it work if you light them again?" asked Martin doubtfully.

"Every bit as well."

The ten candles were reassembled on the remaining sector of cake, and Martin, feeling very self-conscious, stood by while they were relit. His guests were pushed forward.

"All ready? Blow!"

There was a loud puffing. Bunny's blast, a little too late, blew a fragrant waver of smoke into his face.

"Did you wish?"

"Yes," said Martin, "I——"

"You mustn't tell it! If you tell, it won't come true."

But he hadn't wished, yet. He wanted to wait a moment, to get it just right. As the children turned away, trooping toward the door, Martin made one hasty movement that no one saw. With a quick slice of the sharp cake-knife he cut off the tail of the plush mouse. Now it would always serve to remind him of the tailless mice in the room that was no longer a nursery. Then, with the snuff of smoking candles still in his nose, he wished.

B

II

"DEAR MISS CLYDE," wrote Mrs. Granville, "it will be so nice to meet you again after all these years. You can imagine my surprise when I found that the house Mr. Granville has taken for the summer is the old Richmond place, which I remember so well from long ago. Twenty-one years, isn't it? It hasn't changed a bit, but everything seems so much smaller, even the ocean somehow. The house has been shut up a long time, since the summer the Richmonds went away. We want you to join our Family Picnic, which is always an amusing affair. Mr. Granville admires your work so much, I did not realize until recently that you must be the same person I knew as a child. There are other artists here too, the Island has become quite a summer camp for painters, the woods are full of them, painting away merrily. I am sorry this is so late, but just send us a wire saying you can come. . . ."

She paused to reread the letter, and changed "so nice," in the first line, to "nice." She changed "twenty-one" to "nearly twenty." She crossed out "painting away merrily." How do I know whether they're merry? she asked herself. Then she noticed that the word "summer" was used three times. She changed one of them to "year." No, that made three "years." Put "for the vacation" instead of "for the summer." Now the letter must be copied again.

Why on earth George wanted her to invite the Clyde creature when things were complicated enough already . . . she had never cared much for her even as a child . . . to have outsiders here for the Picnic when they had only just got the old house in running order, and Lizzie was overworked in the kitchen, and expenses terrific anyhow . . . George thought Miss Clyde might be the right person to do the pictures for the booklet he was writing for the railroad company. Always thinking of his business first and her convenience afterward. Business was something to be attended to in offices, not to be mixed up with your home life. Never try to make social friends of your business acquaintances, how many times had she told George that?

Damn the Picnic, damn the Picnic, damn the Picnic!

Of course she had only brought down one sheet

of paper; now she must go up again for more. The dining table was the single place in the house she could write a letter. If she halted in the bedroom, in a moment Nounou was at the door with endless this that and the other about the children If she sat down on the porch, Lizzie could see her from the pantry window and would come at once with stentorian palaver. Why couldn't a cook do what she was told, not argue about it? In the little sitting room George had spread out his business papers; anyhow, she couldn't bear him near her when she wanted to write. And in the garden it was too hot. A bumblebee was bumping and grumbling against the pane. If you took a cloth and held him, to put him outdoors, his deep warm hum would rise to a piercing scream of anger. She felt like that. If any one touched her . . .

The bee was fussing up and down the window, the one with red and blue and orange panes. She remembered that window from childhood visits to the Richmonds. When you looked through the orange glass, the purest sky turned a leaden green, dull with menace; the clear northern sunlight became a poisoned tropic glare. And the blue panes made everything a crazy cold moonscape, with strange grapejuice colours underneath the

leaves. It reminded her of George's favourite remark, in moments of stress, that women's conduct
is entirely physiological. Ponderous pedantry!
Vulgar too. Physiology, a hateful word. Suddenly she felt an immense pity for all women
. . . even Miss Clyde. She went up to the
bedroom to get another sheet of paper.

George had actually moved the bureau at last,
so that the light fell justly on the mirror. Yes, the
pale green dress was pretty. Like lettuce and
mayonnaise, George had said, admiring the frail
yellow collar. It brought out the clear blue of
the eyes, like sluiced pebbles. She was almost
amazed (looking closely) to see how clear they
were, after so many angers, so much—physiology.
One can be candid in solitude. Thirty-four.
What was that story she had read, which said
that a woman is at her most irresistible at thirty-
five? Mother had sent it to her, in a magazine,
and had written in the margin *True of my Phyllis.*
She laughed. What a merciless comedy life is.
Ten years before, Mother would have marked in
the same way any story that said *twenty*-five.
Was there no such thing as truth? Blessed
Mother, who knew that woman must be flattered.
A pity that story hadn't been in a book instead of
a magazine. Books carry more authority. . . .

But books, pooh! Who had ever written a book that told the innermost truth? Thank God, in her secret heroic self she was aware of joy and disgust, but she kept them private. Truth is about other people, not about me. A woman doesn't bear and rear three children . . . bring them into the world, a comelier phrase . . . and cohabit with a queer fish like George without knowing what life amounts to. And how enviable she was: young, pretty, slender, with three such adorable kiddies.

"I don't care, there won't be any one at the Picnic prettier. I was made to be happy and I'm going to be."

She hummed a little tune. "Jesus lover of my soul, let me to thy bosom fly." George was vulgar, but he was amusing. When the beetle buzzed down inside her blouse at the beach supper, tickling and crawling so far that she had to go into the bushes to take him out, George said "That must have been the bosom-fly you're always singing about." Sometimes it seemed as though the world was made for the vulgar people, there are always so many ridiculous embarrassments lying in wait for the sensitive. When the wind blew, her skirts always went higher than any one else's. She would wear the new pink camisole at the

Picnic, that fitted very snugly . . . still, a
thing like that bosom-fly would hardly happen
twice. George always wanted to take jam and
sardines on a picnic; sticky stuff that attracts the
bees and ants. Fortunately we're all wearing
knickers nowadays. . , . Poor old blundering, affectionate, and maddening George. Still
it was something to have married a man with
brains. There were so many, so much more attractive, she could have had, as Mother (dear loyal
Mother) often reminded her. It's a good thing
people don't know what mothers and married
daughters talk about. That is the rock that life
is founded upon: an alliance against the rest of
the world. Away off in the future, when her
own daughters were married, she would have
them to confide in. You must have *someone* to
whom you can say what you think. But which of
the three? You can't confide in more than one.
Three little girls, three darling little girls, like
dolls. Thank goodness there wasn't a boy to grow
up like George: obstinate, greedy, always wanting
to do the wrong thing . . . it was enough to
break any woman's spirit, trying to teach a man
to do things the way nice people do them. If
George wanted to lead an unconventional life,
he ought to have been an artist, not gone in for

business. . . . And such a crazy kind of business, Publicity, now working for one company, now for another, here there and everywhere, neither flesh nor fowl nor good red income. A man ought to have a settled job, with an office in some fixed place, so you always know where he is. A country club is a good thing for a husband, too, where he can meet the right sort of men (how handsome they are in those baggy breeches and golf stockings), lawyers and a banker or two, influential men with nice manners. You can always 'phone to the clubhouse and leave word; or drive up in the coupé (it ought to be a coupé) and bring him home to dinner. She could hear voices, voices of young pretty wives (not too young, not quite as pretty): "Who is that in the green dress, with the three little girls all dressed alike, aren't they *cunning!*—Oh, that's Mrs. Granville, Mrs. George Granville, her husband's in the advertising business, he adores her."

Where was the box of notepaper? The children must have been at it, the top had been jammed on carelessly, split at one corner. Of all annoying things, the worst is to have people pawing in your bureau; there isn't any key, of course. How can a woman be happy if she can't even have any privacy in her own bureau drawer? If George ever

wants anything he always comes rummaging here
first of all. The other day it was the little prayerbook.—Why, George, what do you want with a
prayerbook? I thought you were an atheist.—
So I am, but I want to strengthen my disbelief.
I was beginning to weaken.—What a way to talk.
George *is* an atheist, but he believes in religion for
other people: because it makes them more un-
selfish, I dare say. Yet, in a queer way, George
has a pious streak. Perhaps he's really more
religious than I am.—The only thing I have
against God is that He's a man . . . not a
man, but . . . well, Masculine. How can
He understand about the special troubles of women? That must be the advantage of being a
Catholic, you pray to the Virgin. She can understand. But can She? After all, a Virgin . . .
I *mustn't* let my mind run on like this, it's revolt-
ing the things you find yourself thinking.

From the bay window at the head of the stairs,
over the garden and the sweep of grassy hill, she
could see the water. Along the curve of shore, a
thin crisp of foam edging the tawny sand. If she
didn't get off that letter to Miss Clyde it would
be too late for her to come to the Picnic. The
Brooks were coming this afternoon. It was
Nounou's evening off, too. What perfect weather.

B*

This lovely world, this lovely world. Oh, well, if George wanted the Picnic now, she might as well go through with it.

As she went down, George was in the hall, lighting his pipe. He looked very tall and ruddy and cheerful: almost handsome in his blue linen shirt and flannel trousers. An eddy of smoke rose about his head. She halted on the stairs.

"George! Don't puff so much smoke. I want to see the top of your head . . . I do believe it's getting thin."

"How pretty you look," he said. "I like the green shift."

He enjoyed calling things by wrong names, and the word *shift* always amused him. He found words entertaining, a habit that often annoyed her. But this time she did not stop to correct him.

"You ought to wear a rubber cap when you go bathing. The salt water gets your hair all sticky, and then the comb tears it out. I don't mind your being an atheist, but I'd hate you to be bald."

He blew a spout of tobacco smoke up at her. It was extraordinarily fragrant. Oh, well, she thought, he's not a bad old thing. He's endurable.

"George." She intended to say, "I love you." But of their own accord the words changed themselves before they escaped into voice.

"George, do you love me?"

He made his usual unsatisfactory reply. "Well, what do you think?" Of course the proper answer is, "I *adore* you." She knew, by now, that he never would make it; probably because he was aware she craved it.

"I'm writing Miss Clyde to come to the Picnic." He looked a little awkward.

"Needn't do that, I wrote to her yesterday. I said you were busy and wanted me to ask her."

"Well, of all things——"

She curbed herself savagely. She *wouldn't* lose her temper. Damn, damn, damn . . . his damned impudence.

"When is she coming?"

"I don't know yet. To-morrow morning, I dare say."

"Well, then, we'll have the Picnic to-morrow, get it over with."

He began to say something, put out his hand, but she brushed fiercely past him and ran into the dining room. She tore her letter into shreds, together with the clean sheet she had brought down. The room was full of a warm irritating buzz.

"George!" she cried angrily, with undeniable command. "Come here and put out this damned bee!"

III

THE kitchen was hot, flies were zigzagging just under the ceiling, swerving silly triangles of ecstasy in the rising savour of roast and sizzling gravy.

"Lizzie, you *must* keep the screen door latched. There was a big bee in the dining room. That's how they get in.—Where are the children?"

"It's that man, he always leaves it open."

"The ice man? Well, speak to him about it."

"No, ma'am, the one in the garden. The one Nounou took 'em down to the beach to get away from. She didn't think he was quite right."

What on earth was Lizzie talking about?

"A man in the garden? What's he doing here?"

"I gave him a piece of cake. He saw it in the pantry window and asked for some. Then he was in again for a glass of water."

Another problem. Life is just one perplexity after another. But there must be some explanation.

"He asked for a piece of cake? Who is he, the gardener?"

Lizzie was flushed with heat and impatience. Her voice rose shrilly.

"He didn't exactly ask for it, but he was lookin' in the window at it and he says, 'They always give me a piece of cake when I want it.' No, he ain't the gardener. I don't know who he is. I thought maybe a friend of yours, one o' the artists. He was playin' with the kids."

She stepped outside, resolutely attempting not to think. Automatically she adjusted the lid of the garbage can. But the mind insists on thinking. Was it better for the can to stand there in the sun, or to go in the cellar entry where it would be cooler? Sunlight is a purifier: the heat would tend to dry the moist refuse . . . but the sun attracts flies too. She stooped to lift the can, then paused, abandoned the problem, left it where it was. Just like George to have rented an old-fashioned barracks like this, not even gas for cooking. No wonder the place had stood empty for years and years. The idea of cooking with coal in July. If the oil range didn't come soon Lizzie would quit, she could see it in her face. The ice box was too small. If they took enough ice to last through the day, there was no room for the ginger-ale bottles. She had known it would be like this.

The garden seemed to sway and tremble in
brilliant light. A warm sweetness of flowers
floated lightly, the air was not really hot after all.
Why did Nounou let the children leave their
croquet mallets lying all anyhow about the lawn?
Remind George that Nounou's wages will be due
on the twenty-third. If you don't remind George
of those things he complains about being taken by
surprise. Beyond the hedge of rose bushes, a blue
glimpse of water. It *was* a heavenly place.
There must be some consolation in a garden like
this. If one could breathe it in deeply and not
think, not think, just slack off the everlasting
tension for a few moments. Of course it's quite
useless, but I'm going to pray. God, please help
me not to think. . . . In France, Catholics
say *vous* to God, and Protestants say *tu*. That's
rather curious. . . . There, I'm thinking
again. No wonder the artists come here in summer, the Island is so lovely. Loafers, that's what
they are, idling about enjoying themselves making
pictures while other people plan the details of
meals and housekeeping . . . and Picnics.
She could imagine Miss Clyde sitting in the garden
sketching, relishing it all, romping with the children, while *she* was doing the marketing. Are
there enough blankets for the guest-room bed?

And with only one bathroom . . . Miss Clyde is probably the kind of person who takes a terrible long time over her bath.

The strip of beach gravel that led toward the rose-trellis was warm and crackly underfoot. Among the grey pebbles were small bleached shells. Once upon a time, she had told the children, those shells belonged to snails who lived in the sea. When the tide went out, their little rocky pool got warm and torpid in the glare. Then the sea came back again, crumbling over the ledges with a fresh hoarse noise: great gushes of cold salty water pouring in, waving the seaweeds, waking up the crabs. She could imagine the reviving snails wriggling happily in their spiral cottages, feeling that coolness prickle along their skins. She would like to lie down on the gravel and think about this. Would reality, joy, truth, ever come pouring in on her like that? There was a bench in the rose-garden, if she could get so far. When things are a bit too much for one (fine true old phrase: they *are* just a little too much for us, adorable torturing *things*) it's so strangely comforting to lie flat on sun-warmed earth . . . the legend of Antæus . . . but not here, Lizzie could see her from that synoptic pantry window. How large a proportion of life consists in heroically denying the impulse? But just round this corner, behind the shrubbery——

Someone was doing it already. Oh, this must be the man Lizzie spoke of. How very odd: sprawled on the gravel, playing with pebbles. Lizzie must have been right, one of the artists. Unconventional to come into a private garden like that . . . asking for a piece of cake. Never be surprised, though, at artists. Perhaps he's doing a still-life painting: something very modern, a slice of cocoanut cake on a lettuce leaf. Artists (she had a vague idea) enjoyed making pictures of food. But he'd been playing with the children, Lizzie said. What sort of person would play with children before being introduced to their parents? Perhaps he wanted to do a portrait of them. Portraits of children were better done with the mother, who could keep them quiet . . . I always think there's no influence like a mother's, don't you? . . . On the bench in the rose-garden, that would be the place. She could see the picture, reproduced in *Vanity Fair* . . . Green Muslin: Study of Mrs. George Granville and Her Daughters. But even if it were painted at once it couldn't possibly be printed in a maga-zine before next—when? January? George would know about that. But strange the man didn't get up, he must hear her coming. He looked like a gentleman.

"How do you do?" she said, a little coldly.

He was studying the pebbles; at the sound of her voice he twisted and looked up over his shoulder. He seemed faintly shy, yet also entirely composed.

"Hullo!" he said. "I mean, how do you do." His voice was very gentle. (How different from George.) Something extraordinary about his way of looking at her; what clear hazel eyes. Instead of offering any explanation he seemed waiting for her to say something. She had confidently expected a quick scramble to his feet, a courteous apology for intruding. She felt a little angry at herself for not being able to speak as reprovingly as he deserved. But there was a crumb on his chin, somehow this weakened her. A man who would come into people's gardens and ask for cake and not even wipe the crumbs off his chin. He must be someone rather special.

"You're doing just what I wanted to," she said.

He looked at her, still with that placid inquiry.

"I mean lying on the ground, in the sun."

"It's nice," he said.

Really, of all embarrassing situations. If he didn't get up, she felt that in another minute she *would* be sprawling there herself. A very un-

graceful pose for the portrait: Mrs. George Granville and Her Daughters, prone on the gravel.
Women ought not to lie like that anyway, it
humps up the sitting-part so obviously. Yet they
always do in bathing suits, most candid of all
costumes. . . . Perhaps for that very reason.
What queer contradictions there are in good manners. This was too absurd. Thank goodness, he
was getting to his feet. The crumb shone in the
sunlight, it adhered to his chin with some of Lizzie's
sticky white icing.

"Was the cake good?" She meant this to be
rather cutting, and was pleased to see him look
a little frightened.

"Awfully good." Now he looked hopeful, rather
like a dog. She could not altogether understand
the queer way he had of studying her: steadily,
yet without any of the annoying or alarming
intimations that long gazes usually suggest. But
he made no movement to leave.

"I suppose you're waiting for another piece."

"Yes," he said, smiling.

Now, she felt, she had him trapped. This would
destroy him.

"You haven't finished the first."

He understood at once, and ran his tongue
toward his chin until it found the crumb. She

watched it disappear with the feeling of having lost an ally. She had counted on that crumb to humiliate him with.

"All gone," he announced gaily. What could one do with a man like that?

"I suppose you're an artist." Not knowing what else to do she had turned toward the house, and he was walking with her. He was tall and pleasantly dressed and had rather a nice way of walking: politely tentative, yet with plenty of assurance.

"I'm Martin."

Her mind made little rushes one way and another, trying to think if she had heard of him. He must be very famous, to give his name with such easy simplicity. Why do I know so little about art? she asked herself. Well, how can I keep up with things, there's always so much to do. It's George's fault, expecting me to run a big house. If we'd gone to the Inn . . . what are the names of the famous painters? Sargent was the only one she could think of. She could see George at the pantry window. In a moment she would have to introduce them, what should she say? What was George doing in the pantry?

"George, let that cake alone!" she called. It sounded a pleasant humorous cry, but George's well-tuned ear caught the undertone of fury. That was just like George. Whenever he was angry or upset he went to the pantry and got himself something to eat.

"I was saving the cake for the Picnic," she explained.

"A Picnic!" said the stranger. His brown face was bright with interest. "When?"

If George could invite people to the Picnic, why shouldn't she? By the way, I mustn't forget to order some sardines.

"Where are you staying?" she asked.

Apparently he didn't understand this, for he replied, "I don't mind." He was looking at the pantry window, where George's guilty face peered out from behind the wire screen.

"How funny he looks, like a guinea-pig in a cage," he said.

That was exactly what George did look like, squinting out into the sunshine. The end of his nose, pressed against the mesh, was white and red, like a half-ripe strawberry.

"George, this is Mr. Martin, the famous artist. He's coming to our Picnic."

IV

GEORGE was in a fidget, in the little sitting room that opened off the hall. It was just under the stairs and when any one went up or down he could hear the feet and couldn't help pausing to identify them by the sound. It was astonishing how many footsteps passed along those stairs: and if they ceased for a while it was no better, for he found himself subconsciously waiting for the next and wondering whose they would be. He had laid out his maps and papers and the portable typewriter, all ready to begin work: the draft of his booklet on Summer Tranquillity (for the Eastern Railroad) would soon be due.

His mind was too agitated to compose, but he began clattering a little on the machine, at random, just to give the impression that he was working. Why should any one invent a 'noiseless' typewriter, he wondered? The charm of a typewriter was that it *did* make a noise, a noise that shut out the racket other people were making. What a senseless idea, to imagine that he could really get some work done here, buried in the country. He could not concentrate because there was nothing to concentrate *from*. There was only the huge vacancy of golden summer, droning pine trees, yawning beaches, the barren pagan earth under a crypt of air. The world shimmered like a pale jewel with a flame of uneasiness at its core. The place to write about Summer Tranquillity would have been that hot secret little office of his in town, where the one window opened like a furnace door into a white blaze of sunshine, where perspiration dripped from his nose on the typewriter keys, but where he had the supreme sensation of intangible solitude.

What on earth were they walking about for, upstairs? Was she showing the man the whole house? He looked distractedly across the garden. The listless beaming of the summer noon lay drowsy upon the lawn, filling him with an appalling sense of his absurd futility. As Phyllis had so often said, he was neither business man nor artist. What the devil was he working for, what goal was there, what fine flamboyant achievement was possible? He had a feeling of being alone against the world, a poor human clown wrestling with grotesque obsessions; and no longer really young.

He leaned toward the glass-paned bookcase, tilting his head anxiously to see the reflection of the top . . . certainly it was receding in a V above each temple—but that made the forehead seem higher. He had always believed that, among advertising men, he looked rather more intellectual . . . he turned again to the window, a little ashamed of his agitations. Beyond the glass veranda he caught the stolid gaze of the cook at the pantry window. He averted his head quickly: ridiculous that you can't do anything without catching someone's eye. All this was just insanity. He took up the page he was working on and rolled it into the typewriter. Page 38 . . . like himself, thirty-eight, and forty only two pages away. I suppose that at forty a man feels just as young as ever, but . . . it's absurd to feel as young as I do, at thirty-eight. . . . Well, I must keep my mind clear (he thought, rather pathetically)—it's the only capital we have.

Phyllis's footsteps were coming downstairs. He was always worried when he heard them like that: slow and light, pausing every few treads. That meant she was thinking about something, and in a minute there would be a new problem

for him to consider. When he heard them like
that he usually rushed into the hall, demanding
hotly, "Well, what is it *now?*"

"What is what?"

"You know I can't work when you come downstairs like that.'

"Like *what?*"

"As though you were worrying."

"Well, why didn't you take a house where I
could slide down the banisters?"

This time the feet came down so slowly he felt
sure she *wanted* him to rush out. The rushing out
always put him in the wrong. Well, he just
wouldn't. He would stay where he was, that
would show her he was indignant. He took out
page 38, put in a blank sheet and rattled the keys
vigorously. But he felt cheated of a sensation.
He always enjoyed bursting out, through the door
at the foot of the stairs, and catching her trans-
fixed on the landing, with the big windows behind
her—half frightened, half angry. He would not
have told her so, but it was partly because she
was so pretty there: the outline of her comely
defiant head against the light, her smooth arm
emerging from the dainty sleeve that caught and
held a pearly brightness. How lovely she is,
he thought; it's gruesome for her to be so pretty

and talk such nonsense . . . she needs someone to pump her full of indigestible compliments,
that would silence her——

She was at the telephone. He could hear her
talking to the grocer. "I'm sorry, Mr. Cotswold,
is it too late to catch the driver? I've got some
unexpected guests . . ."

He hastened into the hall. "Don't forget the
sardines," he shouted.

She looked at him calmly with the instrument
at her mouth. She seemed surprisingly tranquil.

"Never mind, then, thank you," she said to Mr.
Cotswold, in the particularly cordial and gracious
voice which (George felt) was meant to emphasize
the coolness with which she would now speak to
him.

"If you want sardines you'll have to go down
and get them yourself. The driver's left."

She went into the sitting room and automatically
pulled the blind halfway down. He followed her
and raised it to the top of the window again.
She sat on the couch, and he was surprised to see
a dangerous merriment in her face.

"I suppose you think you can shut yourself in
here and just let the house run itself," she said.
"Like a sardine."

"I have to do my work, don't I?"

She looked at the sheet in the typewriter, on which was written wildly *Now is the time for all good men to come to the aid of this absurd family*. But she did not comment on it, and George felt that this was one of her moments of genius. He wondered, in alarm, what she was going to do with him next. He felt helpless as only a husband can.

"Well, anyhow, they pack sardines in oil, not in vinegar," he said angrily. This sounded so silly it made him angrier still. He closed the door and cried in a fierce undertone, "What's the idea, this man Martin? Who is he? Is he staying for lunch?"

"He's an artist. I thought you liked artists."

"Yes, but we don't have to fill the house with 'em."

"I've put him in the spare room."

"In the spare room! What about Miss Clyde?"

"I haven't the faintest idea. He seemed to expect it, somehow. He's a very irresistible person."

"I guess I can resist him. If we've got to have him in the house we can put him in here, on the couch."

"It's too late. He's in the spare room now, washing his hands.—You needn't have been so rude when I brought him in."

"I didn't like his looks," George mumbled.

This wasn't true. George *had* liked his looks, but he had resented (as must every man burdened with many perplexities) that gay and careless air. He looks as if he didn't have a thing on earth to worry about, George thought. And he comes floating in here, with casual ease, among the thousand interlocking tensions of George's diffi- culties, to gaze with untroubled eye on his host's restless alertness. Or was this some sort of joke that Phyllis was putting over on him?

"I'm going to put the two older children on the sleeping porch, so Ben and Ruth can have their room. Miss Clyde will have to go on this couch."

"How about me?"

"Well, we can sleep together I suppose. It won't kill us, for a few nights."

Not if I know it, George thought. That old walnut bedstead, with the deep valley in the middle, so that we both keep rolling against one another. Unless you clutch the post and lie on a slope all night. Besides, Phyl is so changeable in temperature. When she goes to bed she's chilly and wants to kindle her feet against you. Then by and by she gets warmed up and it's like sleep- ing with a hot bottle five feet long. On a night in July, too. Whenever I get comfortable, she wants to turn over on the other side; that brings us face to face. Impossible! How unexpected life is. If any one had told me, twelve years ago, that it would be so irritating to sleep in the same bed with a pretty woman, I wouldn't have believed it. Phyl doesn't like it either, yet she was annoyed by that booklet I wrote for the Edwards Furniture Company on The Joys of the Separate Bed. I'll sleep on the window seat in the upstairs hall. No: that won't do, if Miss Clyde is in the den she'll have to be coming upstairs to the bathroom and Phyl won't like me spread out there in public. It's funny: sleeping is the most harmless thing people ever do, why are they so furtive about it?

But George rather liked the idea of Miss Clyde on his couch. It seemed, somehow, to add piquancy to a dull situation. To conceal this private notion, he argued against it.

"Miss Clyde will be a long way from the bathroom," he said.

"There's no other place to put her. You're always talking about artists, their fine easy ways, I guess she won't mind if someone sees her in a wrapper."

She'd look charming in a wrapper, George

thought. The queer little boyish thing! I can just imagine her. It would be blue, a kind of filmy blue crêpe. Coming up the stairs the morning sunlight would catch her, through those big windows: her small curves delicately outlined in a haze of soft colour, her hair tousled, a flash of white ankle as she reached the top step. He would sit up on the window seat, as though just drowsily awakened. Oh . . . good-morning! Good-morning. What a picture you would make. Silhouette Before Breakfast. Life is full of so many heavenly pictures. . . . The bay window above the garden would be calm and airy in the before-breakfast freshness of July; the house just beginning that dreamy stir that precedes the affairs of day. She would come across to him . . . he had hardly dared admit, even to himself, how far they had gone in imagination. . . .

"I'm damned if I want strange women careering all over the house in their wrappers," he said with well-simulated peevishness.

"Bosh!" exclaimed Phyllis. "There's nothing you'd like better. Unless without their wrappers."

"What's the use of being vulgar?" he said. He thought: How gorgeous Phyllis is. You can't fool her.

Poor old George, thought Phyllis. I believe he imagines that he's attractive to women. But I won't say that to him, he's in such a stew already.

"Miss Clyde is one of the most truly refined people I ever met."

This didn't quite succeed. Phyllis was always annoyed when George attempted to bunco her. He was so transparent.

"I believe you imagine you're attractive to women," she said.

"Hell," he said, "I don't even take time to think about it."

"If that were true, you'd be much more so."

If I'd finished this cursed booklet, he thought, I'd take a little time off and *be* attractive to women, just to surprise her. Why, damnation, I could even make Phyl fall in love with me if it was worth taking the trouble. The way to please women is to show them that you know they're not happy. And that their special kind of unhappiness is a particularly subtle and lonely one, but curable by sympathy. But it's better not to think about these things at all. It's queer to think of all the people in the world, and how troubled they are when they look each other straight in the eyes. If I knew why that is, I'd know everything. The devil of it is, women have begun to think. That's

why everything is so uneasy. Why even Phyllis
has begun to think. I mustn't let her, because
she's too fond of being comfortable. It'll only upset her. She *must* be kept amused. That's the
beauty of money, it's a substitute for thinking.
It can surround you with delightful distractions.
It's like women, too: it comes to the fellows who
know how to entertain it. I must learn how to be
attractive to money.

"Certainly, Phyl, no one can say that *you're*
attractive to women. You're too pretty." He
leaned over and kissed the end of her nose. There,
perhaps that would calm her, he might still be able
to do half an hour's writing before the children
came back from the beach. That was the only
solution. Simplify, simplify life by burying yourself in some work of imagination—such as the
Eastern Railway booklet. He smiled bitterly.
Those were the only happy people, the artists—
immersed in dreams like frogs in a pond, only their
eyes bulging just above the surface. But how
are you going to attain that blissful absorption?
Dominate the ragings of biology by writing railroad folders? The whole universe turns contrary,
he thought, to the one who wants to create. Time
is against him, carnal distraction, the natural
indolence of man. Yes, even God is against him:

God, Who invented everything and is jealous of other creators. If Phyllis hadn't been there, he would have fallen on his knees by the couch and told God what he thought of Him.

They heard someone coming downstairs. Phyllis rose.

"Come in, Mr. Martin! See the nice little den where George does his work."

V

GEORGE is carving the meat. He always feels better at meal times. The trouble with me, he thinks, is that I take things too seriously. I dare say I haven't any sense of humour. Let's see if we can't make a sort of fresh start from this moment.

The three little girls are brown and gay. Phyllis looks tired, but busily exhibits that staccato sprightliness that comes over her when there are guests. This Mr. Martin seems a silent fellow. The children stare at him, and seem to have some joke among themselves; Sylvia and Rose nudge each other and giggle. I always think it's a mistake to let the two younger ones sit side by side. But Mr. Martin seems unaware of them: his eyes are fixed on Phyllis with a cheerful watchfulness. He's a solemn bird, thinks George, but he has the good taste to admire Phyl. I hope he won't overdo it, for her sake. She can't stand much admiring: it goes to her head right away.

"Well," Phyllis says, "this is really delightful. A distinguished guest is just what we needed to

51

make the Picnic a success. Children, don't kick
the legs of the table.—Mr. Granville is so fond of
artists, he employs such a lot of them in his business. Of course, I dare say your kind of work is
quite different, but there must be a lot of painters
who wouldn't know what to do if it weren't for the
little advertising jobs that come along. We're
so happy to be in the country again. Of course
we live very simply, but Mr. Granville can always
work so well when he gets away from the office.
I feel so sorry for the men who have to be in town
all summer."

George feels a violent impulse to contradict her,
but masters it. Phyl, he says, ask Lizzie to bring
a spoon for the gravy. She always forgets it.—
Mr. Martin, I'll tell you the kind of people we are,
we never have a carving knife sharp enough to cut
with.

"Well, George, it's not our own carving knife.
You see, Mr. Martin, we took this house furnished.
It's not like having our own things."

Our own isn't any better, George's voice shouts
angrily inside his head, but he manages to keep it
from coming out.

Are we going to the Haunted House for the
Picnic? the children ask.

Not unless you take your elbows off the table,

Phyllis says sharply. Mr. Martin, who looks puzzled, takes his elbows off too.

There's a poor old tumbledown farm, on a sandy cliff, among dark pine trees, Phyllis explains. Someone has told the children that it's haunted. The word means nothing to them, but they can tell —by the way people say it—that it suggests something interesting.

Yes, if it doesn't rain, George says. He is too experienced a parent ever to make positive promises.

This would have been a good day for cold meat and salad, he thinks, sawing away at the joggling-slippery roast. Phyllis sees him thinking it. "I'm sorry to have hot meat on such a warm day, but we'll need it to-morrow for the sandwiches. There's some iced tea coming."

"Hot meat to make your inside hot, iced tea to make it cold," the children exclaim. "Do we have to eat the fat?"

They always ask this question. Then Mr. Martin asks it too, which causes amusement. How delightful Mr. Martin is, Phyllis thinks. He has a sort of eagerness to be happy, to enjoy things, to move blithely from one minute to the next. Even George feels it, he looks less cross. But George, as he takes down a tall glass of iced

tea in one draught, is making calmly desperate
resolves. I haven't the faintest idea what anything means, he is telling himself, but I'm just
going to go on placidly. I'll go cracked if I keep
on worrying. Maybe after lunch I can take a
snooze in the garden. One of the little girls
wriggles happily on her chair, her pink frock has
slipped sideways on her smooth brown shoulder,
showing the frilled strap of her shirt. With a
gentle twitch George pulls her dress straight and
pats the child's golden nape. She looks at him
with innocent affection. That little bare shoulder
makes him think of women and their loveliness,
and all the torments of unease to which these same
poor youngsters must grow up. He concentrates
his mind on the blue and white platter, the brown
gravy dimpled with clear circles of fat and turning
ruddy as the juice of the roast trickles down, the
amber tea with slices of lemon. Thank Heaven
Time still lies before them all like an ocean. Even
he and Phyllis are young, they don't need to do
anything definite about life, not yet. Keep your
mind on the small beautiful details, the crackling
yield of bread-crust under the knife, the wide hills
over the sea, sunset on open spaces that evapo-
rates all passion, all discontent. He picks up his
napkin from the rug, helps himself to vegetables,

and begins to eat. How delicious life is, even for an abject fool like me, he thinks. I wonder if any one ever feels old?

"The Picnic is our great annual adventure," Phyllis was saying. "I hope you won't think us too silly, but we *do* look forward to it enormously. It's such fun to forget about things once in a while and just have a good time."

"Yes," said George, "we worry about it for weeks beforehand. And we always invite more people than the house can properly hold."

Phyllis flashed a little angry brightness across the table.

"You mustn't think us too informal if things are a bit crowded, that's part of the fun."

"What is informal?" asked Mr. Martin, quite gravely.

George smiled. Why, the man was kidding her.

"Informal's what women always say they're going to be and never are."

"George loves to lay down the law about women, Mr. Martin. As a matter of fact he knows nothing about them. I expect you know more than he does, even if you're a bachelor."

"Is there a lot to know?" said Mr. Martin.

The man's delightful, thought George.

I never felt as queer as this before, thought

Phyllis. I feel as though something astonishing were going to happen. Or worse still, as though nothing would *ever* happen. How many sandwiches will we need? Three children, two of us, Mr. Martin, Ben and Ruth, Miss Clyde—that makes nine. When this gruesome Picnic is over, perhaps I shall have a chance to ease up. I feel as though I should like to fall in love with someone. I wonder if Mr. Martin would do?

"Mr. and Mrs. Brook are coming this evening," she said gaily. "You'll like them, they're charming."

"As a matter of fact," said George (she always knew, when he began with that phrase, that he was going to contradict her), "they're the dullest people on earth; so completely dull that you can't help envying them. They're the perfect mates, too stupid even to disagree with each other. If every other couple in the world went smash, marriage would still be justified by Ben and Ruth."

"How do couples go smash?" asked Janet.

"You finish your beans and don't talk," said Phyllis.

She was pleasantly fluttered by the way Mr. Martin looked at her. His eyes kept returning from his plate: lingering on her face with a gently inquiring studiousness that was not at all offensive.

I believe he really does want to do a portrait of me, she thought. He's fixing the features in his mind. She turned her head toward Sylvia and Rose so that he would see the half-profile with an appealing madonna softness upon it. The coloured glass panes behind her, what a vivid background that would make.—But she felt he was about to ask a question, and allowed her eyes to come round to meet him, to make it easier for him. Obviously he was shy.

"Do I have to finish my beans?" he said.

What a difficult question to answer. There must be some joke that she did not see.

"Beans make bones," asserted Rose fatuously.

"Why, of course not," she said hastily. "I was afraid that cocoanut cake would take away your appetite." No, that was the wrong thing to say: she saw George's face sharpen at the mention of the cake: he was getting ready to blurt out something and she felt sure it would be awkward. With the speed of a hunted animal her mind dodged in search of some remark that would give her time to think.

"I like the English way of serving beans, slicing them lengthwise, you know; it makes them so tender, without any strings." There; surely that would dispose of the absurd topic. "George, what are you going to do this afternoon? Go for a swim?"

"But these *are* string beans," said George. "They're supposed to have strings. Perhaps Mr. Martin misses them."

"If he doesn't finish his beans, Virginia can have them," Sylvia suggested. "She eats vegetables sometimes."

Virginia was the cat, just now obviously misnamed. Phyllis knew very well what was coming next, but she could not speak fast enough to avert it.

"Beans will be good for her," said Janet with enthusiasm. "She's going to have a family very soon, she needs nourishing food."

"Mother says she mustn't have a shock, it might be bad for the kittens."

"That'll do, never mind about Virginia."

Lizzie was making grimaces from the kitchen door, holding up a cup custard and contorting a red face of inquiry. Phyllis nodded. But perhaps Lizzie means there aren't enough custards to go round? "Oh, Lizzie, put on the fruit too."

George, with his damnable persistence, had not forgotten.

"How about the cake?" he asked.

"George, you know we've got to save the cake

for the Picnic. I can't ask Lizzie to make another one."

"It's been cut already," he said.

I'm *not* going to be humiliated like this in front of a stranger. George is just doing it because he sees Mr. Martin admires me. Will this meal never end? I'm past battling over trifles. Have the cake if you want it. I don't care. If Lizzie puts it on, all right. Leave it to her. I'm not going to order it on. Cooks always take the man's side anyhow. I'm afraid Mr. Martin will think we're lunatics.

"What do you think of a husband that always knows exactly what's in the pantry?" she asked him.

A moment later she couldn't remember what he had said to this. Perhaps it's because I'm so absorbed in my own thoughts. The only thing I really remember his saying was his comical question whether he need finish his beans. It's odd, how much he conveys without saying anything, just by a look.

Lizzie had put on the cake. Phyllis saw at once that there were only six custards. She could tell, by the way Lizzie planked them down, there were no more in the kitchen. If they all took one there wouldn't be any for Lizzie herself, and that would mean bad temper. She refused the custard. She wanted a peach, but felt that the effort of peeling it was too much. Soft fuzzy skin and wet fingers. Then George, with that occasional insight that always surprised her, passed her one peeled and sliced.

"Yes," he said, "we ought to have a bathe, unless there's a storm. Relieve the pressure on the bathroom."

"Then we'll all be nice and clean for the Picnic," exclaimed the children.

"Miss Clyde is coming," George continued. "She's an artist too, perhaps Mr. Martin knows her."

"Bring the jug of iced tea in the garden, let's finish it out there," said Phyllis. "It's stifling here.—Children, you go and get your naps."

The little table was under the pine trees, the other side of the croquet oval. The grove smelt warm and slippery. Now there are the long hours of the afternoon to be lived through, somehow. George sprawled himself on the brown needles, the smoke of his pipe drifted past her in a blue whiff. Mr. Martin put a chair for her.

"I love these pine trees," she said. "They're always whispering."

"It isn't polite to whisper."

She smiled at him. He does say the quaintest things.

"Nature never is polite. On an afternoon like this the whole world seems to yawn in your face."

"These trees smell like cough drops." This was George.

An artist's mind is always on the beautiful, Phyllis thought. She pulled her skirt down a little, and tried to decide what was the most beautiful thing visible, so she could call his attention to it. She wished she hadn't said that about yawning, she felt one coming on. The hot lunch had made her frightfully drowsy. Across the bay thunderheads were massing and rolling up, deep golden purple. "I wish I could paint," she said. "See those wonderful——" But she began the sentence too late; the yawn overtook her in the middle of it.

"Wonderful what?" asked George, looking up. She was struggling with the desire to gape; she trembled with the violence of her effort. George stared.

"Are you ill?"

"Wonderful clouds," she finished savagely. George watched her, adding one more tally to his private conviction that women are mostly mad.

"If you poured heavy cream into a glass of grape

juice," he said, "it would look just like that. Coiling round and clotting."

Sickening idea, Phyllis thought.

"I know exactly what's going to happen, just about the time I have to drive over——"

He was going to say it, she felt it coming. He was going to say *depot* instead of *station*. George always said *depot* when they were in the country, and she couldn't bear it. It was coming, it was coming; everything was predestined; all her life she had known this scene was on the way, sitting under the hot croup-kettle smell of the pine trees, blue thunder piling up on the skyline, poor adorable George mumbling away, and Mr. Martin watching them with his air of faint surprise. It was like the beginning of some terrible poem. Everything in life was a symbol of everything else. The slices of lemon lying at the bottom of the iced-tea jug, on a soft cloud of undissolved sugar, even they were a symbol of something. . . .

"George!" she interrupted desperately. "I had the most terrible premonition. I felt that you were going to say *depot*."

"Why, yes, I was going to say, just about the time I'm ready to drive over——"

For his own sake, for her sake, for Mr. Martin's sake, George must be prevented. If he used that

word, she would know that all this was fore-
ordained, beyond help and hope. With a quick
movement she pushed her glass of tea off the table;
it cascaded onto George's ankle. He paused in
surprise.

"I'm *so* sorry. How careless of me, your nice
white socks, look out, that little piece of ice is
going down inside your shoe."

She felt that the guest's eyes were upon her. He
must have seen her do it. "Is that why they call
it a tumbler?" he said.

"Never mind," said George cheerfully. "It
feels fine. I wish it was down my neck."

For a moment transparent Time swung in a
warm, dull, uncertain equilibrium. Phyllis could
see Lizzie jolt heavily down the kitchen steps and
bend over the garbage can. The grinding clang
of the lid came like a threatening clap of cymbals.
How glorious it would be if she and Lizzie, each
with a garbage can and lid, could suddenly break
into a ritual dance on the lawn, posturing under the
maddening sunlight, clashing away their fury in a
supreme dervish protest. How surprised George
and Mr. Martin would be. She and Lizzie making
frantic and mocking gestures, sweating the comedy
out of their veins, breaking through the dull mask
of polite behaviour into the great rhythms and

furies of life. No longer to be tired out by little things, but to be exhausted and used by some great ecstasy. She was watching every movement life made, and thinking, as it was finished, There, that's over, it never can happen again. But it all *would* happen again, and how weary she was of keeping to herself her heavy burden of secret desires and pangs. Why couldn't she tell George? But if you tried to tell George things, he went far, far away—because, probably, he too had so much that he yearned to tell. You can't really be intimate with people who know you so well. Yet she had never been so fond of him. Here, in this garden, they seemed for an instant secure from the terror of the world. Behind these walls, these burning roses, disorderly forces could not reach them.

Mr. Martin was a comforting sort of guest, he did not talk but just looked happy and was spooning up the sugar from the bottom of his glass. Drink life to the bottom of the vessel, you always find some sugar there, all the more palatable for the lemony taste.

A clear compulsory ringing trilled keenly across the lawn. They listened, unwilling to move.

Then there was the squeak of the screen being lifted in the pantry window. Lizzie put out her

head and called. Phyllis found it impossible to
stir.

"George, you go. Then you can put on some
dry socks."

"Nonsense," he said, getting up. "I'll be lots
wetter than that if the storm breaks while I'm
driving to the depot."

VI

PHYLLIS could feel the whole flat of visible world gently tilting. Equilibrium, if there ad been any, was gone: they had begun to slide. George, receding across the level grass, seemed to descend a downward slope. Martin was lying at ease on the ground beside her, with one knee bent and the other leg cocked across it. Perhaps that's why he's so fond of lying on the ground. It's easier to keep from sliding. He seemed to have forgotten she was there and was humming to himself. She felt he had the advantage that silent people always have over the talkative. But if she could get him into conversation, she could make him realize that she was more thoughtful than she seemed.

"I'm glad you didn't finish your beans," she began.

He did not seem surprised. "I'm glad you're glad," he said presently.

"I don't like finishing things either."

To this he said nothing at all, and she realized that her carefully drilled waggishness, which she kept for callers, would descend upon her in a minute. She struggled against it. She had a forlorn desire to feel real for a few moments, to say things she believed. But of its own accord an archly playful remark popped out.

"Now you mustn't let us bore you, you must feel free to do whatever you want. I think it's dreadful to force guests to be amused."

"I feel awfully free. Don't you?"

This was so unexpected that her mind went quite blank. There seemed no possible reply that was worth making.

"I should like to lie in bed and laugh," he said calmly.

Phyllis tried to think of something to laugh about. It suddenly struck her that there are days when one does not laugh at all. Evidently this was one of them. The world had swinked, and looped its wild orbit for uncountable ages, all to produce this latest moment of lucid afternoon: and yet what cause was there for mirth? But she felt that if she could produce a clear chime of amusement it would be a mannerly and attractive thing to do. She opened her mouth for it, but only managed a sort of satiric cackle.

"You mustn't *try* to laugh," he said. "It's bad for you."

She wondered whether she ought to pretend offence. Of course I'm not really offended: there's something so gently impersonal about his rudenesses. In this dreadful vortex of life that seems to spin us round and round, how amazing to find someone so completely nonchalant, so . . . so untouched by anxiety . . . as though his mind had never been *bruised*. (When she found the right word she always liked to think of it as underlined.)

She had often wondered, hopefully, if she would ever be tempted beyond her strength. Absurd: this was the sort of thing that simply didn't happen to . . . to nice people. But there was a warm currency in her blood, radiant and quivering. She ought to go indoors and lie down . . . lie on her bed and laugh . . . but feeling her knees tremble she remembered that the underskirt was very sheer, and in that violent sunlight, walking across the lawn, he would see an ungraceful bifid silhouette . . . you can't really shock women, but you have to be so careful not to startle men . . . without seeming to pay special attention he was evidently terribly observant. . . . What was it George had said once? that she was so beautiful his eye always enjoyed imagining the lines of her . . . her.
. . . No, *body* is a horrid word . . . her

figure . . . under her thin dress. George was
so carnal. And worse than that, apologetic for it.
Mr. Martin isn't carnal . . . and if he were,
he wouldn't deprecate it.

"All the things I like are bad for me."

She had said this almost unconsciously, for her
mind had gone a long way ahead. She was thinking that if George drove recklessly through a
thunderstorm, and the car skidded, and he
. . . died . . . passed away . . . on
the way to the hospital at Dark Harbour (because
the most appalling things do happen sometimes:
why, once a flake of burning tobacco blew from
George's pipe into his eye, as he was turning a
corner, and the car almost went into the ditch)
. . . what on earth would she do? Wire to
New York for mourning, and would it be proper
to keep Mr. Martin in the house after the funeral?
The little churchyard on the dunes would be
such a picturesque place to bury a husband:
sandy soil, too (it seems so much cleaner, somehow) and harebells among the stones. What was
that kind of lettering George was always talking
about? Yes, Caslon: he would like that—

GEORGE GRANVILLE
IN THE 39TH YEAR OF HIS AGE

Certainly it would never do to have him there after the interment (Mr. Martin, that is). It would have to be at two o'clock so he could get the 3:18 train. Two o'clock makes it rather early, it would interrupt George's nap after lunch. . .

But Mr. Martin was sitting up looking at her with interest.

"Really?" he was asking. "You feel that way too?"

She had forgotten what she had said; and she couldn't very well say "*What* way?" She must have said something rather good, because he was gazing at her with lively expectancy. His inquisitive eyes, eager brown face, were utterly charming. How fascinating human beings are, she thought: their nice fabricky clothes, their queerly carved faces. She wanted to stretch beside him on the shiny needles, let the sun bake and cook away this horrible curdling sickness that shook inside her; purify all her idiocy in the warm clear pleasure of exchanging ideas. Why even animals can communicate their sensations more cordially than people. Must this fardel of identity always be borne alone?

"Yes," she said, with her perfected smile. She wanted to put her hand on his shoulder. to know if he was actual. When the whole fire and anger of a woman's life reaches out for some imagined fulfillment, she finds no luxury of phrase to say her pang. She is a movement of nature, a wind that stirs the grass, a moth blundering in the rain. I shall tell him in a minute, I shall tell him, God help me not to tell him. Is this being tempted beyond my strength? But this isn't temptation, this is just Truth. This was God Himself. Weren't we told to love God? Perhaps George would say that biology was just making fun of her. You're not supposed to love more than one person at a time—not in the same way, at least. . . .

"Even Picnics?"

"Don't speak of the Picnic," she said. "I hate to think of it. Damn the Picnic."

He looked startled.

"George made up a limerick once," she said. "It began like this: *I never believed in monogamy, My husband has just made a dog o' me.* But he couldn't find another rhyme."

"What's monogamy?"

"Something terrible," she said, laughing. This was the real laughter she had hoped for. She seemed lifted, purged, held in a twinkling skein of mirth. Laughter, like flame, purifies. Certainly he was adorable, but she couldn't quite make

him out. Why should he, who evidently enjoyed
horrifying others, be so suddenly aghast himself?
Plainly he was making fun of her: but she could
see he was the kind of person who would not try,
clumsily, to say the things that ought never to be
said. For every woman knows all these things
anyway, and prefers to say them herself.

There was a clatter on the veranda, three serial
slams of the screen door, quick crunching of gravel,
the children. How she loved them, the gay flutter
of their short dresses, the brown slender legs grad-
ually paling toward their soft fat little hams.
They came running across the lawn, knees lifting
and shining in the brilliant light. They surrounded her in a hot laughing group, breathlessly
explaining some plan. Daddy was going to take
them swimming, if there was a storm they could go
into the bath house, it wouldn't matter anyway if
they had their bathing suits on, Daddy would play
Moby Dick the White Whale. The words came
tumbling out of them, they seemed packed with
words, bursting with a vision of green warm water
scalloped with foam, Daddy the White Whale
snorting in the surf, the prickling terror of storm
darkening the sky. What vitality, what career of
the spirit of life!

"Children, children, don't forget your manners. Make a nice curtsey to Mr. Martin."

At once they became well-regulated little dolls. What a picture, she thought: The Curtsey . . . the three children bobbing, their mother in the background, supervising as it were: seeing that Life kept within bounds, did no violence to the harmony of the composition. Because (heavens!) it was bad enough for *her* to feel as she did: she couldn't endure the thought of Janet and Sylvia and Rose growing up to such—such disorders. If they were painted like that, curtseying, of course the pose would be difficult to hold. But all poses are difficult to hold.

"I don't know that I like the idea of your bathing with a storm coming on," she said. That was George, putting wild schemes in their heads. If she forbade it now, there would be tears——

"It's what we're all doing, all the time," said George. He had come quietly across the grass while she was showing the children off to Martin.

This was so surprisingly subtle, for George, she scanned him in amazement. He looked like An Anchor to Windward, A Stitch in Time, Something Put By for a Rainy Day. No one ever looked less like a Leap in the Dark. In short, he looked like a Husband: large, strong, reliable, long-suffering, and uninteresting. The best way to look, probably (she thought), for the interesting people have such a painful time.

"It was a telegram from Miss Clyde," he said. "She's coming this afternoon. Same train as the Brooks."

"This afternoon! I thought it was to-morrow."

There was something guilty about George's shrug. He must have told her to come to-day.

"Well, then, George. You'll have to clean up your den right away. And the Brooks are going into the children's room, that bed has got to be fixed. It's all right for Janet, but that spring'll have to be fixed before Ben and Ruth sleep there."

The children's faces were troubled.

"It's all right, little toads," said George. "You go and get your swim anyhow. Mr. Martin can go with you and be the White Whale. I'll come down as soon as I've fixed the beds."

"I haven't any suit," said Martin.

"All the more like the White Whale," said George. "But you can take mine, it's in the bath house."

The childre , gaily chattering, led Martin off. Phyllis watched them along the hot pebbly path. Beyond the sundial it curved through shrubbery to the green wicket gate. Here, up a grassy gully, came the sharp breath of the sea. In a sort of daze her eyes went with them. That little valley, between the tall dunes, was like a channel through which, if the level garden tilted ever so little, all life would sluice out. When the gate opened it would be like pulling the plug in a bathtub. Everything would begin to flow. With a horrid gurgling sound, probably.

George was beneficently silent. Dreamily she found herself following Martin and the children. If she got as far as that tuft of grass without George speaking, she would not need to answer. She was almost there. She was there. She put her foot squarely on it. Then to her surprise she turned and waited. George was filling his pipe. His silence could only mean one thing: he was frightened about something. She felt her advantage come swimming back into her, a thrilling flutter of strength. Yet she was angry at him for not trying to hold and subdue her.

"Well, why don't you say something?"

He blazed with delighted peevishness.

"At least tell me which bed is which?" he shouted.

"Both of them," she said.

Now the others were hidden behind the shrub-

bery. In a minute they'd be through the gate.
She drifted swiftly after. There was the place on
the gravel where she had found him lying. The
pebbles were still scuffed about. But even if
the gardener raked the path a thousand times she
would never forget that exact spot. They were
at the gate. The children were showing him how
fine it is for swinging on. All was clear in her
mind. She would tell the girls to run ahead, and
as they twinkled down the slope she would turn to
Martin. Her eyes would tell him everything.
. . . No, not everything; but enough to begin
with.

Then, *I love you*, she would say. Softly. She
whispered it to herself to be sure she had the right
intonation. How long was it since she had said
that as it should be said, with amazement and
terror? Ten years? Why, a woman ought to be
able to say it like that—well, every other year
anyhow.

"Don't swing on that gate more than one at a
time," she called. "You'll break the hinges."
And added, to justify herself in Martin's ears,
"Remember, chickens, it's not *our* gate."

They turned, surprised to see her following.

"Children," she began, "you run ahead, I
want——"

The alert, attentive faces of the little girls were too much for her. They gaped over the palings. They knew (she felt sure) that something queer was happening. They always know, as calmly detached as nurses in a hospital who smile faintly at what the patients say under ether.

She hesitated, looking down at her ankles. How trim and orderly they were; when she put on those white silk stockings this morning she had had no idea of all this happening.

She heard the gate clash to, but still paused, her face averted. She wanted her eyes to reach his slowly. For after that it would be too late to plan things. There was a lonely marching in her blood. Then, trembling, she looked.

He wasn't there. He too had run on with the children. All four, far down the hill, romping to the beach together.

VII

GEORGE was fixing the beds, and making an extra-special crashing and clanging about it for Phyllis's benefit, so she would realize how irritating a job it was. I wonder (he was thinking) if any other man ever had to move furniture about so much? Phyllis has a passion for shifting beds. These springs don't fit the frames. The result is that every time any one turns over there's a loud bang, the corner of the spring comes down clank on the iron side-bar. I fixed it—not perfectly, but well enough—with a pad of newspaper and a length of clothesline, when we moved in. Good enough for the children. But of course for Ben and Ruth. . . .

These can't be the right springs for these beds. It stands to reason no manufacturer would be fool enough to send out a bed that couldn't possibly be put together. There must be some trick of arrangement. Human reason can figure out anything, if concentrated on the problem. Now, let's see. This goes here, and this here. Think of having to fiddle over these picayune trifles when the whole of life and destiny is thrilling in the balance. He was lying under the bed now, among curly grey rolls of dust, holding up the spring with one hand while the other reached for the hammer.

Phyllis came in, to empty some of the bureau drawers for Ben and Ruth. She was taking away neat armfuls of the children's crisp clean garments. The whole room was full of their innocent little affairs. There, in the corner, was the collapsible doll house he had made last Christmas, and which had to go everywhere with them. Sitting against the door of the doll house was a tiny china puppet with a face of perpetual simper and that attitude of pelvic dislocation peculiar to small china dolls. Around the house was a careful pattern of shells, diligently brought from the beach. Why did all this make his heart ache? He remembered one evening when he had been working late, he passed gently by the children's door about midnight and heard a quiet little cough. Janet was awake. That small sound had suddenly, appallingly, reminded him that these poor creatures too were human. She must be lying there, thinking. What does a child think, alone at night? He went in, in the darkness, put his arms round the surprised child, and whispered encouragements to her. Jay, he said, Daddy's own smallest duckling frog,

Daddy loves you, don't ever forget Daddy loves you. The little figure sat up in bed, threw her arms round his neck and gripped him wildly in furious affection. "I won't forget, Daddy," cried her soft voice in the warm dark room. Though she was only eight years old her accent was strangely mature: the eternal voice of woman calling man back from agonies and follies to her savage and pitying breast.

Mother love? Pooh (he thought, in a glow of bitterness), what was mother love! A form of self-ishness, most of the time. Of course they love their children, having borne them, suffered for them. Children are their biological passport, their excuse for not having minds. And if they're girls, how mothers hurry to drill and denature those bright dreaming wits. They love them chiefly because they make so pretty a vignette in the margin of their own self-portrait—like a *remarque* in an engraving. But for fathers to love their children—the poor accidental urchins that come between them and the work they love—that really means something!

He gave the bed frame several resounding bangs with the hammer: quite uselessly, merely to ex-press his sense of irritation at seeing Phyllis's pretty ankles and the hem of her green dress mov-

ing so purposefully about the room. Then, looking out angrily from under the bed, he saw her
picking up the shells. Instead of bending over
from the hips, as a man would, she was crouching
on her heels, deliciously folded down upon her
haunches. This annoyed him. And how heartless
to clear away the shells that had been laboriously
arranged in a border round the doll house.

"Why don't you leave them there?" he shouted.
Then he realized how impossible it would be to
explain his feeling about the shells. They repre-
sented innocence, poetry, the hopeful imaginings
of childhood.

Phyllis scooped them up relentlessly.

"Don't be a fool," she said. "You wanted these
people here for the Picnic, didn't you? All right,
we have to make the room decent."

He felt that, as usual, he had picked up the argument by the wrong end. Arguments are like cats:
if you take them up by the tail they twist and
scratch you.

"And another thing," she added. "You simply
must mend that broken railing on the sleeping
porch. If the children are going to be out there
it isn't safe."

"I can't fix *both* these beds," he growled.
"There's a bolt missing. Tell me which one Ben

will sleep in, I'll fix that. Ruth's won't matter,
she's a skinny little thing, doesn't weigh much
more than Janet."

I wouldn't mind so much fixing Ruth's bed, he
was thinking; there'd be a kind of vague satisfaction in that. I rather like to think of her lying
there, she's rather attractive even if she is such a
numbskull. But Ben, that solid meaty citizen
. . . he probably snores . . . I'll tell Ben
to take this one; this is the one most likely to
come down.

"How do I know which will take which?" she
said. "They'll arrange that to suit themselves,
no matter what we say."

He had carefully lashed the spring to the frame
with a piece of rope six weeks before. But it had
worked loose and now must be done all over again.
The deuce of a job: the spring was precariously
balanced at one end only; he was holding the loose
end with one hand, trying to rewind the cord with
the other. The thought of doing all this for Ben
was too silly. No, let Ruth have this one and he
would try to make a good job of it. Perspiration
rolled from him. He supported the spring with
his left elbow, so that he could take the end of the
cord with his left hand while tightening it with his
right. A fuzz of dust was sticking to his moist

cheek. This was too insanely comic: grunting
under a bed on a hot electrical afternoon. He
could see Phyl's feet standing motionless by the
window. How lovely she was, how he wanted her,
wanted to slough away all these senseless tensions
and stupidities. . . . She was always right
because she merely acted on instinct; he, usually
wrong, because he tried to think things out and
act reasonably . . . if she knew how heroic
he really was, would she understand? He *must*
get her to understand before it was too late. For
this—this crisis that was hanging over them, was
his deliberately desired trial of strength. And
now, if they weren't careful, they would fritter
away all their stamina in preliminary scuffle and
nonsense; and when the moment came . . .
soon, appallingly soon . . . there would be
no vitality left to meet it.

He was terrified. He had planned all this,
grimly; now things were moving too fast for him.
A long soft murmur of thunder jarred across the
sky. Would the storm pass over without breaking? No, by God, it *must* break, if they were ever
to find peace. He must send up a kite, like old
Ben Franklin (that first of modern advertising
men) to bring down a sample of lightning. He
must find out whether lightning was the kind of

D

thing you can live with. He must tell her why
he was terrified. He must tell her quickly.
These were the last moments they would have together before . . . already the colour of the
light had changed. Here, on the side of the house
away from the water, there was a darkening sparkle in the air.

Her feet were ominously still. She must be
thinking, and this always worried him. Suppose
she too became aware of this secret insolubility of
life? It was only her divine certainty about little
things that kept him going. What business have
biological units thinking about things? Let them
obey their laws and not question.

Shifting the weight of the spring to his shoulder
he turned over and put his head out from under the
foot of the bed.

"Phyl," he said, "why don't you go and lie
down a bit, have a rest before the folks get here."

She looked down at him. Even in the warm
listless dream that seemed to have mastered her,
she was touched by the foolish appeal in his red,
dust-streaked face. Where the light caught the
turn of his jaw shone a coppery stubble.

"You need a shave," she said; and then regretted her insistent tidying instinct. She was
holding three large shabby dolls, unconsciously

pressing them against her like an armful of real
babies. One flopped forward over her arm, uttering an absurd bleating squawk. *Maaa-maa!*

"The children," she exclaimed breathlessly.
"The storm's coming. Hurry up with those beds;
get the children back from the beach."

"They're all right," he said sulkily. "Mr.
Martin'll take care of 'em."

His large flushed face, mouth open, gazed up
from the floor. He looked pitiably silly, like a
frightened dog. He was thinking, all I want to
tell her is that I love her; no matter what happens
I love her. But how can I say it? If she weren't
my wife I suppose it would be so much easier.
Why do we always show our worst side to the
people we love?

She was thinking: The absurd idiot, writhing
about under that bed like a roach, telling me to go
and lie down when there are a hundred things to be
done, beds to be made, towels and linen got out,
silver counted, instructions to Lizzie. . . .
Certainly she had tried to warn him. . . .

"Damn Mr. Martin!" she cried. "Don't trust
him. You fool, you fool. Can't you see he's
crazy? We're all crazy. Stop sprawling there
like a mud turtle, *do* something."

"Listen, Phyl," he said heavily. "I want to

tell you something. Now, listen, you've got to
help me."

With a pang of alarm he knew that now it was
too late to go back. He had begun to speak.
Now he must try to explain the pillar of smoke and
fire that had moved so long before the lonely track
of his mind. Greatly as he feared her rigid spirit,
he must divide the weight of this heavy fragile
burden, like a crystal globe that might contain
either ecstasy or horror. He could not know
which until it lay broken about him in shining
scraps and curves. But oh, why was she so difficult to tell things to?

"Don't laugh," he mumbled. "It's terribly——"

He wriggled forward earnestly. The other end
of the metal spring slid from its joist, the head and
foot of the bed toppled inward. With a clanking
brassy crash the whole thing collapsed about him.

He lay there, covered with bed, in a furious silence which was merely the final expression of his
disgust. For an instant, in the stillness following
that ridiculous clamour, she thought he was hurt.
She bent down, dropping the dolls, and one of
these again shrilled its whining protest. His angry
face reassured her, and she burst into a peal of
laughter.

He crawled out from under the wreck. He was thinking savagely, yet with relief also, how close he had been to telling her. But that was his fate. Even noble tragedy, if it came near him, would be marred by titters. He didn't blame her for laughing. Even in an agony he could never be more than grotesque.

"I was just thinking," she said, "how awful if the bed did that when Ben's in it."

"Don't worry. It probably will."

Sultry blue air pressed close about the house, air heavy with uncertain energies. He knew now how frail are carpentered walls and doors, how brittle a box to guard and fortify weak things he held dear. A poor cardboard doll house, and his own schemes just a ring of shells about it. Here, in a home not even his own, among alien furnitures, he must meet the sorceries of life, treacheries both without and within. Strong walls, strong walls, defend this rebel heart! he whispered to himself— startled and shamed to find himself so poetical. Strange, he thought (hastily reëdifying the bed), that people spend such anguish on decisions that don't really matter. But in this house he was at a disadvantage. He had no memories in it. For Phyllis it had old associations and meanings. It went back into her childhood, into that strange

time when he had never known her; when she must
have been so cunningly caught unawares and
machined into rigidity. So even the house was
against him. In that charged air, one spark surely
would sheet all heaven with flame. It would be
queer to split open the world's old shingled roofs
and rusty-screened windows, scatter the million
people with little pig-eyes of suspicion, explode
love and merriment over the land. God help us,
he thought, people can't even sin without finding
dusty little moral justifications for it. This is
what civilization has brought us to!—But what a
way for a man to be thinking, with a half-written
booklet on Summer Tranquillity lying on his desk.

He stepped onto the sleeping porch, where two
cots had been put for Janet and Sylvia, to look at
the broken railing. Projecting above the veranda,
it overlooked the garden and the pale sickle of
beach, distinct in glassy light. He could see Martin and the children, tiny figures frolicking on the
sand. The sky was piled steeply with swollen
bales of storm, scrolls of gentian-coloured vapour.
But it looked now as though the gust would pass
overhead. Phyllis was busy at the linen closet by
the corner of the passage, getting out clean towels
and napkins. He envied her the sedative trifles
that keep wives sane. And after all, perhaps the

well-drilled discipline of human beings would
get them past this eddy. People—and especially
guests—know so well what can be done and what
can't. They know how to "behave." The world,
brave prudent old world, is so sagely adjusted to
avert or ignore any casual expression of what men
really feel: terror and mockery, pity and desire.
Oh, surely, by careful management, they could all
shuffle through a couple of days without commit-
ting themselves and then safely relapse into the
customary drugged routine. Ben and Ruth, ac-
complished students of petty demeanour, would
be a great help. Even Joyce, poor bewitched
rebel with frightened eyes, even Joyce must have
some powers of concealment. But he would not
think of Joyce for a little while.

"I think maybe the storm'll blow over," he
called. He felt he must speak to Phyllis again, to
calm his own nervousness.

There was no answer. Going to the end of the
passage he saw her standing at the big bay window
in the spare room. She was looking down toward
the beach, one hand nervously plucking at a strip
of wallpaper that had come loose along the frame
of the window. He crossed the room quietly and
kissed the back of her neck, with a vague idea that
this would help to keep her from thinking. It was

so enormously important that she should be calm
and humorous just now.

He was prepared for silent indifference, or even
an outburst of anger; but not for what happened.
She turned silently and flung her arms madly about
his neck. "Love me, love me, love me," she cried.
"Love me, before it's too late."

He was horrified. "There, there," he said, embarrassed. "Go and rest a while, little frog."

VIII

THE beach was a different world. Under the plum-glossed wall of storm the bay was level, dusky, and still, crumbling in low parallels of surf. The waves collapsed in short flat crashes. The children flashed in the warm dull water: they wore three tight little green bathing suits: their legs so tanned it seemed as though long brown stockings were snugly drawn above their polished knees. They tumbled with the soft clumsy grace of young animals and were happy without knowing it. Janet could swim; Sylvia still used water-wings to buoy her up; Rose preferred not to go beyond knee-depth and squatted in the curl of the small breakers. When the backwash scoured the sand from under her insteps, leaving a hard mound beneath her tickling heels, she squeaked with ecstatic fright. "The ocean's pulling me!" she cried, and squattered to safety. Sylvia, paddling splashily a little farther out, with a white rubber cap and the bulbous wings behind her shoulders, was like a lame butterfly that had dropped from the dunes above. She put a foot

D*

down and couldn't touch bottom. This alarmed
her and she hastily flapped herself shoreward. A
wave broke on her nape, shot her sprawling into
the creamy shallows. The wings spilled off, she
rolled sideways and under with legs flying, her nose
rubbed along soft ridges of sand. Her face, emerging, was a comic medallion of anxious surprise.
Another spread of lacy green water slid round her
chin. She was relieved to find herself laughing.

"A wave went right over me and I didn't mind,"
she exclaimed. "I'm a little laughing girl, and
laughing girls are different."

It was all different. In this width of sky and
sea and sand nothing was reproached. Nounou
was off for the afternoon and could not forbid them
to play with the stranger. Farther along the bay
were other cottages, other children; but here they
were alone. "Do you see those houses?" said
four-year-old Rose to Martin, pointing to the
bungalows that stood on a bluff, sharp upon naked
air. "People live there, with beds and food."

Yet they did not even know they were alone.
Merely they existed, they were. They were part
of the ocean, which does not think but only fulfil
its laws. Tides curve and bubble in, earth re-
ceives them, earth lets them ebb. Soft shells pul-
verize. hard shells polish, sand-hills slither, sea-

weeds dry and blacken: the bay takes the sea in
its great arms and is content: and inland the farm-
yard dogs, those spotted moralists, are scandalized
by the moon. The moon—chaste herself, bright
persuasion of unchastity in others. For life is all
one piece, of endless pattern. No stitch in the vast
fabric can be unravelled without risking the whole
tapestry. It is the garment woven without seams.

Here was beauty; and they, not knowing it, were
part of it unawares. Here was no thinking, merely
the great rhythm of ordered accident, gulls' wings
white against thunder, the electric circuits of law
broken by the clear crystal of fancy. And the sea,
the silly sea, meaningless, prolific, greatest of lovers, brawling over the cold pumice reefs of dead
volcanoes, groping tenderly up slants of thirsty
sand. The sea that breeds life and the land that
breeds thought, destined lovers and enemies, made
to meet and destroy, to mingle and deny, marking
earth with strangeness wherever they embrace.
The sea, the bitter sea, that makes man suspect he
is homeless and has no roof but dreams.

Janet, who was big enough to go beyond the low
surf and grapple the White Whale in his own element, liked Mr. Martin because he did not talk
much and understood the game at once. When
she harpooned him he rolled and thrashed in foam,

churning with his flukes as a wounded whale
should; and came floating in so they could haul
him to land and cut him up for blubber. This, she
explained, is the flensing stage, marking out a flat
area of moist sand. Then they burned the blubber
in a great bonfire, a beacon that glared tawnily
in the night, to guide the relief ship to their
perilous coast. Martin found it ticklish to be
flensed, so they lay and made tunnels. The tide
was going, the flat belt of wet beach was like a
mirror, reflecting the rich sword-blade colour of
the West.

But Martin was a little puzzled.

"What did you say your names are?" he asked
again.

"Janet and Sylvia and Rose," they said, delighted at his stupidity. For it is always thrilling
to tell people your name: it proves that you too
belong to this important world.

Still, this didn't account for the other, the fourth
one. He had seen her watching them from the
beach, and then she had been playing with them
in the tumbling water. He had thought the children just a little bit rude not to greet her when she
joined them. She was not as brown as they, so
perhaps she was a stranger who had newly arrived.
But now, when that heavy thunder rolled like

wagon wheels across a dark bridge of clouds, and the other three ran off to the bath house to dress, she was sitting there beside him.

She was older, but he knew her now. Her face was wet; but of course, for she had been wriggling in the surf like a mermaid. He felt a trifle angry with her: she had got ahead of him, then. He was opening his mouth to speak when she asked him exactly the same thing:

"How did *you* get here?"

He must be careful: if he told her too much she might give him away. She never could keep a secret.

"I've always been here," he said. "It isn't fair for you to tag along. Go home."

Then he realized it was no use to talk to her like that. Why, she seemed older than he: she had even begun to get soft and bulgy, like ladies. But she looked so frightened, he took her hand.

"We can't both do it," he said. "They'll find out. Bunny, you're not playing fair."

"I am, I am!" she cried. "I'm not playing at all. *You* go away. You'll be sorry."

It was awful to see her look so anxious.

"You used to be a laughing girl," he said, "and laughing girls are different. What's happened to you anyway?"

She gazed at him strangely, with so much love in her face he felt she must be ill.

"This is no place for you," he said firmly. "Here among strangers. You'll be lonely. *I* can't look after you."

"They aren't strangers. Oh, please go back before you find out."

This was all senseless and annoying; yet he was sorry for her too. I know what's the matter with her, he thought. He accused her of it.

"No, no!" she said piteously. "No, Martin. Not that. I nearly did, but not really."

"I dare say it wasn't your fault," he said; and then, remembering a useful phrase, "You'll have to excuse me now." He saw Mr. Granville approaching down the sandy ravine. "Here's one of them coming."

"Tell me," she said quickly. "Do you like them?"

"Why, yes, they're nice. They're a bit queer. They seem to worry about things.—They like *me*," he added proudly.

He could see Mr. Granville waving to them to take shelter in the cabin. The bay was already scarred with the onset of the squall.

"Hurry!" Martin said. "Come on, we'll wait in the bath house until the storm's over." They ran together, stumbling up the heavy sand, she lightly, not dragging behind as she usually did. When he reached the door, pulling it open against the first volley of the rain, it was not her hand that he held, but a cold smooth shell.

IX

ONE drawback about Pullmans (Ruth was thinking) is that the separate chairs make it difficult to talk. And she was getting restless: if she didn't say something pretty soon she would begin to feel uncertain of herself. The long melancholy howl of the engine, the gritty boxed-up air (still smelling of the vaults under the Grand Central Station), the hot plushy feel of the cushion prickling under her knees, the roll and swing of the car, the dark ridges of hills, everything was depressing and tedious. Ben was still absorbed in the morning paper—already stale, she thought, for the afternoon sheets were out by now. She had skimmed the magazines, a little irritated by the pictures of interiors of wealthy country houses. She wished that such articles would also include photographs of the number of servants necessary to keep things so perfect. Of course it was easy enough for people like that to have a Home in Good Taste: they just call in a decorator and he fixes everything. But you yourself: how are you going to know what is really Good Taste?

Styles change so. As for the fiction, it sounded as though it was written by people with adenoids. You could hear the author biting his nails and snuffling. She had cleaned out her vanity box, thrown away some old clippings and a dusty peppermint and stubs of theatre tickets. And still Ben was lurking behind a screen of print. Certainly he was the most stay-put of men: place him anywhere and there he would remain until it was time for the next thing to happen.

She began filing briskly at her nails. Presently the newspaper rustled uneasily. She leaned forward and rasped sharply, her soft hand moving as capably as a violinist's. The little sickening buzz continued, and Ben folded the paper lengthwise and looked round it like a man at a half-open door. His brown eyes were large and clear behind tortoise-shell glasses. His eyebrows were delicately poised, ready to rise, like guests preparing to get up from their chairs. In his waistcoat pocket were two fountain pens, one black and one with silver filigree on it. He looked faintly annoyed. Whatever he looked, he always looked it faintly: dimly, sluggishly, somewhat. He was a little bit stout, a little bit bald, a little bit tired, a little bit prosperous. *Littlebit* had been his nickname when she fell in love with him and thought

him such a passionate fellow. She used to like
the name, but had put it out of her mind when she
found it too true. Everything about him was
rather, except only his eyes. They were quite.
In them, sometimes, you saw a far-off defiance.
Something that had always retreated, slipped behind corners, stood warily at half-open doors, but
by caution and prudence, not by timidity. Something that went while the going was good.

"Ben," she said. "Did you see that girl sitting
at the next table in the diner? The one in the
black hat. She came in just before we left."

He thought a moment. "No," he said. "I
was looking at the bill."

"She went through here a while ago. She's in
the day coaches, I guess, because this is the last of
the Pullmans."

No, thought Ben, this isn't the last of the Pullmans, there's another one ahead of it. I noticed
it specially when we got on: it's called *Godiva* and
reminded me to ask Ruth if she'd brought her
bathing suit.—But he refrained from correcting
her, waiting patiently to hear what was coming.

"Of course, I'm not sure, it's so long since I've
seen her, ages and ages, but I think it was Joyce
Clyde."

Ben made a polite murmur of interested surprise,

allowing his eyebrows to stretch themselves a little and pursing his lips gently to show attention. But the name meant nothing to him.

"I shouldn't wonder if she's on her way to the Island too. You remember, she was there one summer when we were all children. I wouldn't have known her, but I saw her picture in a magazine not long ago. She's some kind of artist, I think. She always was a queer kid."

Ben's recollection of old days on the Island was mostly limited to a strip of yellow shore. He remembered catboats and knife-edged grasses, a dock with barnacled piles, learning to make a half-hitch in wet ropes, and the freckled, gap-toothed faces of some other small boys. He remembered splintery plank walks among masses of poison ivy, the puckered white feet of a man who had been drowned, the sour stink of his aquarium of hermit crabs, dead because he forgot to change their water. He remembered an older boy who taught the small fry obscene rhymes. The cheerful disgusting hazards of being young were now safely over, thank goodness. The orderly exacting routine of business was enough to keep a man amused. Twenty-one years is a long time: yet turning the focus of memory a little more sharply he caught an unexpected glimpse of a friendly fat waitress at the old wooden hotel who used to bring him bowls of clam chowder; and some of the grown-ups were still visible. But the small girls seemed to have evaporated, fogged out. Even Ruth herself. He could only recall a distant shrilling of hide-and-seek played after dusk among the sand-hills, the running flutter of pink cotton dresses. Why don't little girls wear pink nowadays, he wondered.

"Did she wear a pink dress?"

"Gracious, I don't know. She had green eyes and was awfully shy. If that *was* her, she's turned out more attractive than I would have thought. Funny, she hasn't bobbed her hair: I thought all artists were supposed to do that."

Ben wasn't greatly interested. His private conviction was that the party would be a bore anyhow: but he couldn't very well return to the newspaper while Ruth was talking. He took off his glasses and polished them.

"What does her husband do?"

"Her husband? She hasn't got one. I suppose she's wedded to her art. I don't think she's the type that's attractive to men."

Ruth regretted this when she had said it, because obviously a little deduction on Ben's part would have led him to her real thread of thought. But he showed no sign of animation, patted her knee in a soothing, proprietory way, and settled his coat round him like a dog coiling for another nap.

"We'll soon be there," he said.

"I hope so. I'd forgotten it was such a long ride. It'll be strange to see the Island again. What a queer thing, George getting hold of the old Richmond place. It's been empty a long time, the family never went back to it after the little girl (what was her name?) died."

As though plunging into a tunnel the train drummed into a squall. Grey slants of rain thrashed the windows, there were heavy explosions of sound. Ruth was usually afraid of storms, but this one seemed to make the long green car comfortable. The smooth hum of the train softened the jagged edges of thunder. She would have liked a woman there to talk to about Joyce. She had been cheerful in the certainty that her own hat was the smartest on the train until Joyce (for certainly it was she) entered the dining car. That curly black felt, with what an air she carried it. There was something gipsyish about her: something finely unconscious in her way of enjoying her lunch while every other woman was watching her. Women run in a pack and hasten to ally themselves against any other who seems to have secret funds of certainty. Those who live from hand to mouth

are always indignant at a private income.   Ruth
knew Joyce at once as one of the lonely kind.
While she had been sitting there, apparently idle
and half asleep, she had turned her chair to command the aisle and was waiting intently to see her
come back through their car.

The delicious resentment that some women at
once rouse in others!   By deep specialized instinct
every woman in the car looked up as the girl went
by.   Sitting there for several hours they had tac-
itly constituted themselves a microcosm of Society,
and now with professional shrewdness took stock of
the alien.   No sculptor, no practised sensualist,
could have itemized her more fiercely.   She was
not "pretty," but in some strangely dangerous
way she was foreign to their comfortable coward-
ice.   She was still untamed, unbroken.   It was
not fair, thought the plumper ladies (though unaware they were thinking it), that a woman of nu-
bile age should still combine nymphlike grace with
the gay insouciance of a boy.   She was carrying
her hat in her hand, and the dark twist of her un-
cropped hair annoyed them as much as, not long
before, it would have annoyed them to see it short.
They marked the flexile straightness of her figure,
the hang and stuff of the skirt, the bend of foot and
ankle; exactly appraised, by the small visible slope

of stocking, the upper curves unseen. They noted the unbroken fall of her dark suit from armpit to hem as she was swung sideways by a swerve of the train and threw up one elbow to keep her balance. The ruddy young brakeman, meeting her just then, steadied her politely with his hand. She smiled as frankly as a lad. She didn't even seem humiliated, Ruth thought, at having to pass through all these Pullmans on her way to the day coaches.

But there was something deeper than that— something she couldn't profitably discuss with Ben. With the clairvoyance of woman she saw, and resented, a creature somehow more detached and more determined than herself. In a vague way, for which no words were possible, she recognized a spirit not more happy but more finely unhappy; a spirit concerned with those impassioned curiosities of life which Ruth knew existed and yet knew not how to approach. She felt the shamed envy and anger that some bitter listener in the audience always feels toward the performer. There was something in that dark childish face and alert reckless figure that made Ruth feel soft and frilly and powdered with sugar. The girl was possessed by some essence, had some fatal current passing through her—something which, if generally admitted, would demand extensive revision of the comfortable world. That was it, perhaps: she looked as though she knew that things most women had agreed to regard as important, didn't really matter. The Pullman microcosm resented this, as an anthology of prose would resent a poem that got into it by mistake. The only satisfaction it could have, and the explanation of its pitiless appraisal, was the knowledge that this poor creature too was mocked and fettered with a body, subject also to the dear horrors of flesh.

With a sense of weariness and self-pity Ruth turned to the window and saw, far off, the hard blue line of sea. They were emerging from the storm, the train hummed and rocketed over marshes and beside reedy lagoons still prickled by the rain. On that horizon lay the memory of childhood to which she was now returning. The chief satisfaction of revisiting juvenile surroundings is to feel superior to that pitiable era: to appear, before one's old companions, more prosperous, circumstantial, handsome, and enviable than they might have expected. But now even her gay little woollen sports hat seemed to have lost its assurance. What right had a mere illustrator (and riding in a day coach) with something proud and eager in her face, to start all these troublesome thoughts? She remembered that even as a child

Joyce never really joined in their games but watched apart with a shy unwillingness: a shyness which, if rubbed too hard, could turn into bewildered rebellion. Ruth was always so intensely conscious of the existence of other people that a merely random speculation as to what her friends were doing could prevent her all day long from concentrating on her own affairs. Others were more real to her than herself. Now she was painfully haunted by that look of conviction and fulfilment on the girl's face. Joyce looked unhappy (she consoled herself a little with that); but it was a thrilling kind of unhappiness: an unhappiness scarcely to be distinguished from ecstasy.

She pondered about this, wondering if *she* had ever looked like that? One of her secret anxieties was that she herself was not passionate. Was that, she sometimes wondered, why she and Ben had never had children? In her absorption she practised an expression on her face . . . "rapt" was the word that occurred to her to describe it. Ben, reappearing from behind the paper, was alarmed by her appearance and offered her a soda-mint tablet from the little bottle in his waistcoat pocket.

The dense air of the car began to be alive. After the barrens of pinewood and long upgrades over

stony pasture, now the train careered gloriously in
the salty northern air, along beaches crusted with
stale foam   It cried aloud, its savage despairing
chord: as though the fierce engine knew that after
all its furious burning labours, the flashing uproar
of its toil, its human employers would descend at
their destinations unfreed, unaltered, facing there
as elsewhere the clumsy comedies of life.   Angrily
it exulted along the bright dwindle of rails which
spread wide under the great wheels and narrowed
again before and behind.   The telegraph poles
came racing toward it, leaping up like tall threatening men; one by one they were struck down and
fled away.   With swift elbowing pistons and jets
of silver steam the engine roared, glorious in its
task; glorious in its blind fidelity and passion, car-
ing nothing that all must be retraced in the oppo-
site direction to-morrow.

Joyce was standing in the vestibule of *Godiva,*
smoking a cigarette.   She had been there a great
part of the journey; fast trains always made her
mind too busy for sitting still.   She had pacified
the at first disapproving young brakeman by getting out her sketchbook and making a quick car-
toon of him.

Not for many weeks had she been so unconsideringly happy. She never thought of trains as hurrying toward something but rather fleeing wildly *from*. Those great eloquent machines (she hated to have to board a train without seeing the engine first) crouched ready for flight like huge beasts breathing panic. They were symbols of the universal terror; she trembled with excitement to feel the thrill of escape—escape from anything. Escape, for the moment, from Time and Space. She wondered how any one could ever sleep or be bored in a train. You'd think their faces would be transfigured when they got out. She hummed to herself as she stood alone in the vestibule. Life seemed to be beginning all over again: her mind was freshly sensitized to the oddity of human faces, to the colour and vitality of the country, the strong swelling curves of the hills. I am flying, flying, she chanted; I am flying from a dream. I am a little mad. My mind is fuller than it'll hold: all sorts of thoughts are slopping over the brim, getting lost because there isn't room for them. I must let them flow faster so I can be aware of them all. What happens to the thoughts that get spilt before you can quite seize them? I must ask George. . . . I wonder which George it will be?

Once she had startled him by giving him a book

she found in a second-hand store, *The Four Georges.*
For it amused her to insist that there were four of
him: George the Husband, George the Father,
George the Publicity Man, and then George the
Fourth—*her* George, the troubled and groping
dreamer, framed in an open window. . . .

Go and see Granville, said the Advertising Agent
to her. He's getting up a booklet for the L or
somebody. He might be able to use some of these
drawings of yours. And because it was urgent he
had given her the address. Her knees were quiv-
ery as she turned the bend in the corridor, looking
for his number.

It was a sultry day, the door of the little office
was open. There was a window, high up at the
back of the old building, looking over the Brooklyn
Bridge. He was leaning on the sill, the smoke of
his pipe drifted outward into that hot tawny light
that hangs over the East River on summer after-
noons. At first he did not seem to hear her tap
on the glass panel; then he turned, glanced at her
steadily and without surprise. As he had no idea
she was coming she thought perhaps he had mis-
taken her for someone he knew.

"Look here," he said, "I want to show you
something."

She put down her folder of drawings and crossed
to the sill. He leaned there in his shirt sleeves,
pointing with the stem of his pipe, as easily as
though they were old friends.

"See those tall lance-headed openings in the
piers of the Bridge? Did you ever notice they look
just like great cathedral windows? And that
pearl-blue light hanging in them, better than any
stained glass."

She was too surprised, too anxious about showing him her drawings, to do more than murmur
assent.

"I can tell you about it," he said, "because I
don't know you. It isn't safe to tell people you
know about beautiful things. Those are the windows of my private cathedral."

How often she had lived again that first en-
counter. The ring of feet along the paved corri-
dors, the blunt slam of elevator gates, the steady
tick of a typewriter in an adjoining office, tele-
phones trilling here and there in the big building
like birds in an aviary, the murmur of the streets
rising up to them through warm heavy air. Always, in that city, she was a little mad. Where
such steep terraces cut stairways on sky, where
every tread falls upon some broken beauty poets
are too hurried to pick up, how can one be quite

sane? God pity the man (George said once) who
has none of that madness in his heart.

I have a cathedral too, I have a cathedral too,
she was repeating to herself, but too excited to say
it. With bungling fingers she untied the portfolio,
rummaged through the drawings, found the one of
an aisle of trees in Central Park where the wintry
branches lace themselves into an oriel.

He went through all the pictures. He only
spoke twice.

"Who did these? You?" and then presently,
"Here, this isn't fair. You've been trespassing in
my city."

Then suddenly he paused, flushed, and became
embarrassed. He became—as she would have
said afterward—George the Third. He spoke of
the Elevated Railroad's limited appropriation for
promotion, of the peculiar problems of transporta-
tion publicity, asked what was her usual price for
art work, took her name and address. . . .
Perhaps George the Fourth would have died then
and there, perished of cholera infantum at the
age of half an hour, never been heard of again except on a tablet in the imaginary cathedral on
Brooklyn Bridge . . . but as she left the
office she shook so with purely nervous elation she
had to stop by the brass-rimmed letter chute in

the hall. She was wishing she had the courage to go back and ask him how soon the check could come through (Will he mail it here? she thought. Oh, blessed chute!) . . . and then he came hurrying round the corner after her.

"Look here," he said, with pink-browed uncertainty, "I can't let you go away like this. The family's off in the country. I'm devilish lonely. Will you have dinner with me and we can talk about New York?"

She was too amused and exultant to answer promptly. But George the Fourth, looking anxiously from his bassinette, need not have been so afraid she was going to refuse. Do artists who have just made their first real sale decline a square meal?

"We'll ride uptown in the L, to celebrate," he pleaded. "There's a bit where it turns right into the sunset for a few blocks; if you stand on the front platform it's corking. And I know a place where we can get a bottle of *asti spumante.* . . ."

The lighted candles of the Italian basement where they dined. At first his shyness had come back upon him: he seemed to feel that taking any one but Phyllis out to dinner was an incredible truancy. Then, as they looked anxiously at each other, some element in the blood broke free. His mind came running to her like a child, like a boy lost in a world of tall stone buildings and clamouring typewriters. His poor shivered ideas just fitted into the fractured edges of her own. He had been well drilled, but there was in him a little platoon that had broken away from the draft and enlisted in the Foreign Legion.

"You know," he said, "I never talked like this to any one before. What is there about you that makes one say what he really thinks? My mind feels as though someone had stolen its clothes while it was in bathing. How will it be able to go back to work to-morrow?"

Warm golden candlelight and cold golden wine: the little table in the corner was a yellow island in a sea of cigarette smoke, a sunny silence in the comforting hum of other people's chatter. In her own loneliness she saw his mind like the naked footprint on Crusoe's beach.

There must have been another footprint there too: the footprint of a mischievous godling who runs the beaches of the world as naked as Man Friday.

"The ideas I folded neatly and hid under a stone" (she could still hear him saying it, there was something delightfully heavy in his way of saying *stone*), "the ideas I thought you have to leave behind when you go bathing in the river of life, I think maybe I shall go back and look under that stone for them and see if they aren't the most important of all. I thought they were just clothes. Maybe they were my bathing suit."

The figure of speech wasn't quite limpid. There was perhaps a little *asti spumante* in it, and a few gassy bubbles of exaggeration. But she understood what he meant. Ten, eleven years older than she, how young he seemed.

He paused awhile, getting younger every moment. He waved away a drift of smoke.

"You must meet Phyllis," he said.

Then he had found, later, that it wasn't necessary, for she had known Phyllis as a child. How small the world is, he said sadly. "Phyllis and I were small, too," she replied.

She wondered if there were four Phyllises also?

"Ten minutes to Dark Harbour," said *Godiva's* porter, coming into the vestibule with his whisk brush. She hardly noticed him dusting her, she was thinking of George the Fourth, the perplexing phantom she had accidentally startled into life. She felt for him a strange, almost maternal ten-

E

derness; an amusement at some of his scruples, an admiration at the natural grace of his mind when he allowed himself to be imaginative. But behind these, a kind of fear: for George the Fourth had grown gigantic in her dreams; sometimes, in panic, she realized how much she thought about him. He was so completely hers because he was hidden in the securest of hiding places—inside a person who belonged to someone else. So she couldn't resist the invitation to go down to the Island, to renew memories of childhood . . . and the most interesting of those ghostly children, she thought, would be George the Fourth, only twelve months old. She had had to remind herself, sometimes, that the first three Georges did belong to others . . . but if you have to keep reminding yourself of a thing, perhaps it isn't so. For the amazement had been mutual. She had awakened George the Fourth, but he had awakened someone too. . . . And frightened by these thoughts (it had been her lonely pride to stand so securely on her own feet) she was flying from the dream of George to George himself—and Phyllis.

Over the wide sea meadows the train sounded its deep bluster of warning: a voice of triumph, a voice of pain, announcing reunions that cannot unite, separations that cannot divide. And George Granville—all four of him, at that moment—driving over the long trestle to the mainland, heard it from afar, and in sheer bravado echoed the cry with his horn.

X

IN THE bathtub Phyllis wondered, for the first time in her life, whether she was "literary." She sat soaping her knees and revelling in coolness that came about her waist in a perfection of liquid embrace. She found herself—perhaps because her eye had fallen on the volume in the den, while she and George were bickering—thinking about Shakespeare. Now, in an intimate understanding that many an erudite scholar has never attained, she perceived what the man with a beard was driving at. The plays, which she had always politely respected as well-bred women do respect serious institutions, were something more than gusts of fantastic tinsel interspersed with foul jokes—jokes she knew were foul without understanding them. They were parables of the High Cost of Living—the cost to brain and heart and spirit of this wildly embarrassing barter called life. The tormented obstreperous behaviour of his people was genuine, after all: they were creatures in a dream, like herself; a dream more true than reality. She could have walked on in any of the plays and taken a part without sense of incongruity. She felt as if she were a phantom in one of the pieces: a creature in the mind of some unguessable dramatist who had mysteriously decided to make a change in the plot. She thought how she and her friends had sometimes sat through Shakespeare matinées, subconsciously comforting themselves with the notion that real people don't behave that way.

Why, Bill, you poor old devil (she said to him), how you must have suffered to be able to write like that. It made her feel quite tranquil by comparison. But of course her own particular absurd-, ities had special kinks in them that were unique: even He would have been surprised. But he would have understood.

A soft flow of air had begun to move after the storm. The big maple tree, just outside the bathroom window, was gold-plated in the dropping sun. The window was above the bath and the ripple of those gilded leaves reflected a gentle shimmer into the porcelain tub. Her shiny knees were glossed with pale green light. Shakespeare would have liked that. She fished for the soap, which slipped round behind her like a young thought.

I suppose that as long as I was 99 and $\frac{44}{100}$ pure

I never could appreciate him. But I don't know whether I altogether enjoy people who understand so well. That's the trouble about George: he's getting weirdly acute, poor soul. Now, Mr. Martin: he looks divinely sympathetic, but I don't think he quite . . . People wonder why one always confides in those who don't understand. But of course! To confide in people who *do* is too terrible. Giving yourself away—yes, exactly: you no longer are keeper of your own gruesome self. That's why the Catholic notion is so sound: confession to God is nothing at all, you know He doesn't care. But to confess to a priest . . . golly, that must take courage.

She lay down for one last lustral wallow, closing her eyes with a calm sensation of new dignity and refreshment. The cool water held her in peaceful lightness, lifting away whatever was agitated and strange. For a moment body and spirit were harmoniously one, floating in a pure eddy of Time. I feel like a nun, she thought. She rose, trickling, threw the big towel round her shoulders, and studied herself in the long mirror. Really, I'm not much more than a child, she mused happily, admiring the slender, short-haired figure in the glass. Or perhaps I feel like a harlot . . . a courtesan, nicer-sounding word. Discarding the

towel she struck a humorous parody of the Venus
Aphrodite attitude, and then felt a little shocked.
She could feel her cheeks warming. She remembered George's coarse remark when they saw the
statue. "It's no use," he said. "Two hands
can't do it. Any one as timid as that needs three."
She sang a little refrain, trying different tunes for
it. She couldn't remember whether she had heard
it, or just made it up:

> *What did Mrs. Shakespeare do*
> *When William went away?*

The soft flutter of maple leaves outside the
window was like a soothing whisper. From the
other side of the house she could hear the click of
croquet mallets and balls. Time for the children
to have their supper, or they won't be finished
before the others get here. Thank goodness it
was cooler, Lizzie wouldn't be so harassed. Wrapping her silk kimono round her, she looked out of
the window. Lizzie's flag was still flying. With
a rough delicacy of her own, the cook did not like
to run out her private washing on the family
line, so she had strung a cord from the kitchen
door to a branch of the maple tree. There, floating like a hoist of signal buntings, were Lizzie's
personalia: all the more conspicuous for her mis-

taken modesty. They were indeed (it was George who had said it) like a string of code flags: a blue apron, a yellow shirt, a pair of appalling red breeches. George always wanted to know to whom Lizzie might be signalling with these homely pennants. They *are* a kind of signal, Phyllis thought. A signal that life goes on, notifying any other household within eyeshot that here too the humble routine of kitchen and washtub and ironing board, of roof and meat and sleep, triumphs in the end over the wildest poet's dream. Shakespeare would have relished them, and been pleased to see these bright ensigns hoisted so frankly in the yellow air.

Dressed in a gauzy drift of white and silver, she paused at the cushioned bay windows by the head of the stair. Her body enjoyed the mixed feeling of snug enclosure and airy freedom which is the triumph of feminine costume. Even her inward self shared something of this sensation: within the softly sparkling raiment of thought she was aware of her compact kernel of identity—tranquil for the moment, but privately apprehensive and alert. On the oval grass plot Martin was playing croquet with the children. Janet, nicely adjusting two tangent balls with a bare brown foot, gave them a well-aimed swipe. Phyllis heard the

sharp wooden impact and Martin's cry of good-
humoured dismay as his globe went spinning across
the turf, leaving a darker stripe on the wet lawn.
It bounded over the gravel and into the bushes,
right by the corner where she had first seen him.
She watched him chase it, lay it on the edge of the
turf, and drive it back. How graceful he was!
He raised his head with a little unconscious lift of
satisfaction as he watched the ball roll where he
wanted it to lie.

A film seemed to have been skimmed from her
eyes. Perhaps it was that level stream of evening
light: the figures moved in a godlike element of
lustre: every motion was perfect, expressed the
loveliness for which life was intended, was unconscious and exact as the movements of animals.
They were immersed in their game as though
there were no past, no future: she felt she could
watch them for ever. Martin's face, gravely in-
tent, bent over his ball. She saw the straight
slope of his back against the screen of shrubs.
The mallet clicked, there was a sharp tinkle as the
ball went through the middle hoop, touching the
little bell that hung there. How can any one look
so charming and yet be so hard to talk to?

Through the scooped hollow of the dunes, catching tawny sparks from the sand, violet dazzles from

E*

the sea, the cleansed radiance of sunset came pouring in. The children's bare legs splashed in
brightness as though they were paddling; honey-
coloured light parted and closed again about their
ankles, the wet shadows dripped and trailed under
their feet. The house, growing dusky, was a dyke
stemmed in the onset of that pure flood. It
caught and held as much darkness as it could; the
rest went whirling out. As if in answer to the
little croquet bell, the old clock in the hall whirred
and jangled six hoarse clanking strokes. They
eddied a moment and then were whiffed away by
the strong, impalpable current that seemed to be
sweeping through. You could tell, by the dull
sound, that the gong was rusty. No wonder, a
house by the seashore, empty so long.

After the cough of the clock silence came up
the shaft of the stairway. Not themselves alone,
but the house too, had its part in everything. She
could feel its whole fabric attentive and watchful,
and wondered how she could have been heedless
of this before. A house of ugly pattern, with
yellow wainscots and fretsawed mantels and panes
of gaudy glass: but she guessed now, what one can
only learn under strange roofs, how precious houses
are. And how wary they have to be, fortresses

against fierce powers, sunshine, darkness, gale. Life has flowed through them: clocks have chimed, logs crumbled, stairs creaked under happy feet. These whispers are all they have to treasure: if you leave them alone too long they get morbid, full of sullen fancies. She remembered herself, visiting that house as a child, once seated at this same window, watching others play croquet . . . *was* it memory, or only the trick of the mind that splits the passing instant and makes one live it twice?

"Come, children!" she called from the window. "Time for your supper."

She went slowly down the stairs. Be calm, be calm, she said to herself; this too will pass; this isn't Shakespeare but only the children's supper time. But the flow of her blood warmed and quickened as water grows hot while you wait with your hand under the bathroom faucet. On the landing, where a shot of sunlight came arrowing through from the sitting-room window, she waited to adjust a slipper. She could hear them on the gravel outside. If he came in now he would find her just so, gilded and silvered like a Christmas card. But their voices remained on the veranda where the children's meal was laid. She could **not** afford to wait long. Now, now, were a few precious moments. This was a dream: and dreams must be recorded at once or they vanish for ever.

She heard one of them sneeze. It was Janet: she knew all their sneezes and coughs by ear. Yes, they probably *have* caught cold, bathing in that storm. And they have to sleep outdoors tonight, too: on the porch, because of this infernal Picnic. It's much colder; the thermometer must have dropped twenty degrees. She hurried to get the sweaters from the cupboard under the stairs.

They were sitting at the veranda table, with milk and bread and jam. Mr. Martin was in the fourth chair. He looked as though he too was ready for supper.

"Well, chickabiddies, did you have a good bathe? I hope you didn't catch cold. Here, put on your sweaters."

They looked up at her gaily. Their upper lips were wet and whitish.

"How pretty you look!" exclaimed Janet.

She had meant to toss him a brief, clear, friendly little gaze; an orderly hostess-to-pleasant-guest regard; but this from Janet startled her. She could see that he was holding her in his eye, meditating the accuracy of Janet's comment. She did not feel ready to face him.

"Thank you," she said lightly. And added, "Wipe your mouths after drinking."

"He says that's a milk moustache," cried Rose, gesturing to the visitor. "It makes you healthy."

Phyllis made a clucking reproach with her tongue.

"You mustn't point. It's not polite to say *he*. Say 'Mr. Martin.' Jay dear, after supper run and put away the mallets. I've told you, I don't know how often, not to leave them lying on the lawn. . . . Oh, not *you*, Mr. Martin. Janet'll do it after her supper."

But he was up already and gone to get them. I suppose this perpetual correcting sounds silly to him, she thought. But how can I help it? George never disciplines them.

"It makes him hungry to watch us eat," said Sylvia. "He wants some supper."

"He's joking with you. We'll have ours by and by."

She followed him into the garden. As she put her crisp silver slipper on the tread of the veranda steps she saw how the foot widened slightly to carry her weight. How terribly I'm noticing things. Something flickered at the corner of her eye: she suspected it was Lizzie, at the pantry window, trying to attract her attention. A throng

of trifles jostled at the door of her mind, tapping
for admission. Probably the ice has given out,
after such heat. Well, then, they'll have to do
without cocktails. I can fix the sandwiches to-
night when everyone's in bed. If it turns chilly
there won't be enough blankets. Nounou won't
be back until late, I must get the children started
to bed before . . . I *won't* think of these
things.

He had put away the croquet implements.

"Thank you. We've just time for a little
stroll before the others get here.—I hope you'll
like Mr. and Mrs. Brook. They're extremely
nice, really, but a bit heavy."

"Perhaps they eat too much." He said it with
the air of one courteously offering a helpful sug-
gestion.

She had wanted, wanted so to be alone with
him: she had a desperate feeling that there were
urgent things to be said, and now she could
utter nothing. Her mind ran zigzagging beside
her, like a questing dog, while she tried to steer
their talk into some channel of reality. Her
thoughts kept crowding massively under her uneasy words, pushing them out before they were
ready, cutting into her speech like italics in a page
of swarthy Roman type.

"We all eat too much in hot weather, I dare say. *Oh, if I could only write him a letter I could make him understand. He's so sophisticated, I suppose the quaint things he says are his way of making fun of me. Why did I suggest our walking like this? You can't see a person's face when you're walking side by side. And if we go round the path again, Lizzie will get me from the pantry.* Let's sit down on the bench."

"It's wet, it'll spoil your pretty skirt."

Skirt! . . . What a word for this mist of silvery tissue she had put on specially for him. . . .

"So it is. Well, let's see what the storm has done to the roses."

The little walk under the trellis was flaked with wet petals.

"Poor darlings, there's not much left of them now. *If Shakespeare was here I should feel the same way. Speechless. Why, he's like a god: lovely to think about, impossible to talk to. He doesn't give anything, just absorbs you: you feel like a drop of ink on a blotter.* I have a horrid suspicion that the ice has given out, you mustn't mind if your cocktail is warm."

He kept looking at her in brief glances. Each time she met them it was like getting a letter in

some familiar handwriting but stamped with a
strange postmark.

"Are they better cold?"

I give up, I give up. It's no use. I can't even
think. There's some sort of veil, mist, between us.
He is a kind of god. He's brightness, beauty.
Every movement he makes is a revelation and a ques-
tion. How can I speak to him when all I want is to
love him. There's nothing earthy, nothing gross
about this. It's lovelier than anything I ever dreamed
of. And if I tried to tell any one it would sound
like tawdry farce. . . .

Dimly she divined what lay between them,
what always lies between men and gods, making
them such embarrassed companions—the whole
of life, the actual functions of living; the sense of
absurdity (enemy of all tender beauty); trained
necessities for silence, that darken the intuitions
of the soul.

It's as impossible as—as the New Testament. I
feel like Christmas Eve: there's a new Me being born.
You can't have a Nativity without pangs. And not
even any one to bring me frankincense and
myrrh . . .

She stopped, picked one of the late rosebuds,
and put it in his lapel. She checked a frightened
impulse to tell him that she named the baby Rose

because it was her favourite flower and she looked
so like a rosebud when she was born. This was
courage, because to say it would have carried on
the doomed conversation one paragraph farther
in safety. To any one else she would have said
it. But now she spoke shakenly, from far within.

"You're not easy to talk to—Martin."

His face changed, he looked less anxious. He
took her hand. She found herself not surprised:
it seemed entirely natural. She felt his fingers
lace into hers. Just as Janet does, she thought.

"I get frightened when people talk to me," he
said.

She looked at him, worshipping. The bad spell
was broken. Instantly she felt they could communicate. He was frightened too—the precious!
Over his shoulder she caught sight of the little
old-fashioned weather vane on the stable, a gilded
galloping horse with flowing tail. Always racing
in blue emptiness and never getting anywhere.
Like Time itself; like this marvellous instant, so
agonizingly reached, that could never come again.
No one who knew her in her daily rote would
quite have recognized her then as she looked into
his eyes. She was completely herself, born again
in innocence, in the instinctive yearning for what
she knew was good. The unknown ripeness of

woman woke for an instant from its long drug of peevish days, small decisions, goaded nothings. Humbled, purified, bewildered, she saw the dark face of Love, the god too errant for heaven and who suffers on earth like a man.

"Martin, I love you."

"I love you too," he said politely.

Beyond the stable she heard the sound of the car.

XI

I
T WAS just adorable of you to come."
Ruth was getting out of the car. They kissed.

"Why, Phyllis! How sweet you look! Gracious: I thought this was a Picnic, and here you are in a dance frock. For Heaven's sake lead me to hot water. Those awful Pullmans; I'm simply speckled with cinders. I feel gritty all over."

That, of course, must be Miss Clyde, on the front seat.

"How do you do! After all these years! I don't suppose we'd have known each other. But we ought to, George admires your work so much."

They shook hands. It was a hard, capable little hand, calloused like a boy's. Phyllis knew now that she remembered the grey-green eyes: agates, gold-flecked, with light behind them. Eyes softly shadowed underneath, as though from too much eagerness to understand; eyes dipped in darkness. The small shy child of long ago, who stood apart from games. How many strange moments had both been through since last they met?

133

George was getting out the suitcases. He was afraid to watch Phyllis and Joyce greet. When a finely adjusted balance hovers in equilibrium you don't breathe on the scales.

"We were on the same train," cried Ruth, "and never recognized each other."

Ben felt the twinge of anxiety common to the husband who hears his wife tell an unnecessary fib. Ruth had said this once before already, in the car, so perhaps it was important. Her allusion to Pullmans, also, was based (he suspected) on the erroneous notion that Miss Clyde had ridden in a day coach. But he liked to back Ruth up, if he knew what she was heading for.

"I guess we've all changed," he said mildly. "The old house hasn't, it looks just the same."

"Miss Clyde's brought her paint box," George said. "She's going to do a picture."

"Oh, yes, and we have another—why, that's fine, Miss Clyde—we have another artist here too, Mr. Martin. You must all come in and meet him."

She stood holding the screen door aside, welcoming them in. George, coming last, saw how her cheerful smile faded to expressionless blank when the guests had passed. She had relapsed into automatic Hostess. How lonely she must be to look like that. I wish it was over, he thought.

His mind felt like a spider that has caught several large flies at once: the delicate web was in danger of breaking.

They entered the hall.

"It isn't changed a bit!" Ruth said. "Exactly as I remember it—except it seems smaller. That old table, for instance, that used to be just enormous. Well, hot water first. I can sentimentalize much better when I'm clean."

George was thinking: Ruth's probably the kind of woman who always twists the toothpaste tube crooked, but her babble will help us around corners.

"I hope Miss Clyde won't mind being in the little sitting room downstairs: you see we're just camping out here, you must all make yourselves at home."

Joyce tried to frame some appropriate reply to Phyllis's clear, faintly hostile voice. She was in the tranced uneasiness of revisit. Coming from the station she had been trying to realize the Island again: her mind was startled by the permanence of the physical world. Things she had not thought of for so long—things that she had apparently been carrying, unawares, in memory—were still there, unaltered, reproaching her own instability. The planks of the station platform, the old scow

rotting in the mud, the road of crushed oyster
shells, the same vacancy of sand and sky.

In the car she and George were both achingly
mute. There seemed to be a sheet of glass between them. The Brooks emitted cheerful chatter
from the back seat, George replied with bustling
geniality, his only mask. How wonderful if they
could just have made this ride in silence; she had
a feeling that all sorts of lovely meanings were
escaping her. There was the notch of blue light
where the road slipped over a prickling horizon of
pines. How just right were the slopes of the
puppy-coloured sand-hills, the tasselled trees
against the pure lazy air, the coloured veining of
the fields. Now, now; here, here; I'm here and
now, she had to remind herself. It's God's world,
whatever that can mean. Golly, you must be
careful how you make fun of religion: it's a form
of art. She imagined a painting of that aisle of
sandy road, climbing through the tall resiny grove.
Religion would be a good name for it.—George
had never seemed so far away as now when she
sat beside him. Would it always be like that?
Oh, teach yourself not to love things, she thought.
Be indifferent. It's love that causes suffering,
it's tenderness that weighs heavy on the heart.
How ridiculous to say that God loves the world.

He doesn't give a damn about it, really. That's why He's so cheerful . . . such a competent artist. His hand doesn't shake. Still, I don't think I want to meet Him. It's a mistake to meet artists you admire; they're always disappointing.

"I shouldn't have come here," she said. "I love it too much. Those trees. They look so surprised. I have a guilty passion for pine trees."

Driving the faithful car had strengthened George. Even the paltriest has an encouraged sense of competence with that steady tattoo underneath his feet. The artist that lay printed like a fossil in George's close-packed heart—the artist that only Joyce had ever relished—always responded to the drum of the engine. He adored the car; when he drove alone to the Island (sending the family by train) he sang to her most of the way. This was *his* guilty passion. Now it was the car's rhyming vitality that came to his rescue. He broke the glass. He cut himself, but he got through.

"Any kind of love is too much," he said.

Then he was grieved to find himself uttering such a cheap oracle; but it comforted Joyce because she saw it was a symptom. It showed that he was trying to tell the truth. She did not dare look at him: she was too conscious of the others behind them, who seemed as massively attentive as an audience in a theatre. Then in a wave of annoyance, Surely I have a right to look where I want? She did so. She could see the confidential tilt of his eyebrow so plainly, she knew he was hers for the taking. Nothing but themselves could stand between them.

"How queer: that's just what I was thinking," she told the eyebrow.

"Oh, do you believe in telepathy?" chirped Ruth. "Ben sometimes knows exactly what I'm thinking without my saying a word."

It can't happen often, George thought.

"What were you laughing at?" he found time to ask her, as the others were descending from the car.

"I was just thinking, there's not much danger of my meeting God, because I'm not pure in heart."

"Oh, I shall be perfectly comfortable anywhere," she said.

The single swathe of sunshine carved the hall, dividing it into two dusks as the word *Now* divides one's mind. All, all unchanged: the series of hemispherical bronze gongs at the dining-room door, the wakeful asthma of the tall clock, the wide banistered stairway with its air of waiting to creak. The soft, gold-sliced shadow trembled with small sounds, and light voices of children drifted down from above. If this was still real, then what was her life of to-day? Why pretend any longer to make the world seem reasonable? It was all a delightful ironic farce with an audience applauding the wrong moments and the Author gritting his teeth in the wings. What use was Time if it availed so little?

The broad stream of sunlight flowed through the house like a steady ripple of Lethe, washing away the sandy shelves of trivial Now, dissolving little edges of past and future into its current, drawing all Time together in one clear onward sluice. What are we waiting for, she wondered. What is everyone waiting for, always? She was painfully aware of George standing near her. It was not silence that sundered them, but their grotesque desire to speak.

"George," Phyllis was saying, "you give Ben a drink or something while I take the ladies——"

In the shadow beyond the table there was a clicking sound. Through the wide opening of the dining-room double doors two figures crawled, on all fours, with a toy train. Janet was in her pyjamas, ready for bed. Martin's hand moved the engine across the floor. They came into the stripe of sunset.

"Wait a minute!" cried Janet. "Here's one of the passengers."

"Put him in," said Martin. "And then the train goes round a sharp curve and smashes into a lot of people, bing!"

"Quick, I'll telephone for a nambulance. You adbretized Perfect Safety on this railroad. It said so in your booklet."

"Well, if people will sit down for a Picnic right on the main line——"

"Goodness, what a nasinine thing to do."

"They were using the hot rails to fry their bacon on."

"Here's the doctor. Are there any children hurt?"

"Children all safe," said Martin, looking carefully through the wreckage. "A lot of grown-ups badly damaged."

"Here's the pistol. Put them out of their misery."

"Bang-bang-bang!"

"They didn't suffer much. I'll go for the wrecking train."

"Janet!" exclaimed Phyllis. "What are you *doing*, running about the house in your pyjamas. And you've got sniffles already."

The two players looked up; but they could see nothing outside their tunnel of brightness. The voice seemed like imagination.

"Of course the railroad company will have to pay money for those valuable lives," said Martin regretfully.

"I'll get the blocks, we can build a norphan asylum for the surveyors."

"Not surveyors, survivors."

"Janet! Say good-night to Mr. Martin and run upstairs."

This time the command was unmistakable. Janet became aware of tall ominous figures emerging from the surrounding dusk.

"Good-night!" she cried hastily, and ran.

"I'm afraid Janet's manners are terrible," Phyllis said. "She ought to have shaken hands, but I don't like to call her back now, she'll catch more cold."

Two other forms appeared at the top of the stairs.

"Is to-morrow the Picnic?" they called anxiously.

Martin was still sitting on the floor, musing over the disaster. Janet halted halfway up and shouted. "He says you said Damn the Picnic."

Sylvia and Rose burst into snivels. There was a moment of difficult pause. Martin realized that something was happening and began collecting the train.

"You *promised* the Picnic for to-morrow," he said, looking up from where he was kneeling.

"Yes, yes, to-morrow, don't worry," George shouted to the children.

"Mr. Martin's been awfully kind at keeping them amused," said Phyllis. "Mr. Martin, Mr. and Mrs. Brook, Miss Clyde.—George, turn on the light, Mr. Martin can't *see* us."

The button clicked, the bulbs jumped to attention, mere loops of pale wire beside the orange shaft of sun. Martin scrambled suddenly to his feet.

"How do you do," he said.

"What stunning towels," Ruth remarked as Phyllis was pointing out the hot-water tap. The embroidery of Phyllis's maiden initials was luxuriously illegible, in some sort of Old High German character. "Surely those didn't come with the house?"

"No; they're mine; all that's left of my trous-
seau. What George calls my pre-war towels."

But Ruth was too busy in her own thoughts to
pursue little jokes.

"Your artist man is rather extraordinary," she
said. "Why should any one so attractive need to
be so bashful?"

"He's not really bashful.—There, I think you'll
find everything you need."

The light twinkled on a tray of yellowish glasses
on the sideboard. George unlocked the cupboard,
took out a bottle, and split open a new box of
cigarettes with his thumbnail. There's a consolation in having these small things to do, he
thought. Meanwhile, what am I really thinking
of? I suppose she's washing her hands. It's
awkward having her downstairs. She'll want to
change. . . . I don't believe she's got a mirror in there. We can hardly expect her to use the
bookcase panes.

"Excuse me a moment," he said. "Ben, pour
the tonic. It's good stuff." Mr. Martin was
still standing by the door uncertainly, holding the
toy engine. Heavens, does the fellow have to be
moved round like a chess man? He's so difficult
to talk to, somehow. George made a cordial

gesture, indicating that Mr. Martin might as well join Ben at the sideboard. Martin crossed the room obediently.

The anxious host glanced into the sitting room. Yes: Phyllis, with her usual skill, had turned the desk into a dressing table: there was a fresh doily on it, a vase of flowers, and the mirror from his own bureau upstairs. Already, though she hadn't entered it yet, the room was no longer his but Joyce's. It had become private, precious, and strange. Here, in the very centre of his own muddled affairs, was suddenly a kernel of unattainable magic. Why in God's name had Phyllis put her in his room? It was too savagely ironic. In my heart, in my mind, in my very bed, and I can't even speak to her. It's too farcical. If I didn't have to keep it secret we could all laugh about it. Secrecy is the only poison.

He carried in Joyce's suitcase and paint box, put them on the couch, and fled.

"Well, Ben, I saved my last bottle for this party. It'll help us live through the Picnic. Mr. Martin, aren't you drinking?"

"What is it?" asked Martin.

"Try it and see. You don't need to worry. It's real."

Ben held up his glass, prolonging anticipation.

The fine vatted aroma of the rye cheered his nostrils. Here at least was one trifle which helps assuage the immense tedium of life.

"Funny to see the old place again," he said. "How well I remember those coloured panes. Well . . ."

"Never drink without a sentiment," said George.

"All right: stained glass windows."

"Good enough. Stained glass windows."

"Is this your first visit?" Ben began politely; but the other guest was still coughing and gagging. His eyes were full of tears.

Not used to good stuff, George thought. You don't get much of this genuine rye nowadays. He and Ben waited, rather embarrassed, until the other had stopped patting his chest. Ben lit a cigarette and blew a ring.

Martin's face brightened. He put out his finger and hooked the floating twirl.

"That's lovely!" he said. "How do you do it?"

Ben was pleased at this tribute to his only social accomplishment.

"Why, it's quite easy. Get a big mouthful of smoke, purse your lips in a circle, like the hole in a doughnut, and raise your tongue suddenly to push the smoke out."

"Do it again."

Ben looked so comic, shaping his mouth, Martin couldn't help laughing.

"You look like a catfish. Can *you* do it too?"

"Not so well as Ben. Gosh, didn't you ever see any one blow smoke rings before?"

"No. My father doesn't smoke."

Ben looked a little perplexed. He had an uneasy feeling that perhaps the artist was making fun of them in some obscure way.

Phyllis called from the stairs. "George, will you come up and speak to the children? They want to be reassured about the Picnic."

"Do I have to finish this medicine?" Martin asked.

George grinned at him, rather tickled by this drollery.

"You must do as you think best. Make yourselves at home, you fellows. I'll be back in a minute."

"Don't you like it?" said Ben.

"No."

"Well, I can help you."

"It was nice of you to blow a smoke ring to amuse me."

There was silence, which Ben concluded by taking the other glass of whisky.

"Happy days," he said.

"To-morrow will be a happy day," Martin said. "We're going to be reassured by a Picnic."

"Have a cigarette," was all that Ben could think of.

"Who were the ladies you brought with you?"

"Well, one of them's my wife."

"Which, the pretty one?"

Ben poured himself another slug. He felt he needed it. He had a strong desire to laugh, but there was sincere inquiry in Mr. Martin's eyes. He really wanted to know.

"Ask *them*," he said.

Phyllis came into the room.

"It'll soon be dinner time. You people all ready?"

Martin held out his arms. It was so nearly the substance of her dream, she moved forward to enter his embrace. Ben's face of surprise checked her in time. She took Martin's hands.

"Mr. Martin is my guest of honour," she explained lightly.

"He seems to be," said Ben, and finished his glass.

They stood a moment. Then Martin said, "You didn't look at them."

"At what?"

"My hands. I mean, are they clean enough?"

F

Janet and Sylvia were already in the two cots
on the balcony; but their eyes were waiting for
George, with that look of entreating expectancy
worn by those who look upward from bed.   In the
lustrous garden air crickets were beginning to
wheedle.   The rickety old porch seemed an alcove
of simpleness divided from the absurd tangled emo-
tions of the house.   But even here was passion:
the little white trousered figures sprang up, their
strenuous arms clutched him, their eyes were
dark with anxiety.   With horror he saw how
they appealed to him as omnipotent all-arranging
arbiter.   Him, the poor futile bungler!   They
crushed him with the impossible burden of their
faith.

"Yes, we'll have the Picnic to-morrow.   Now
you go to sleep and get a good rest."

"Mother forgot to hear our prayers."

He stood impatient as they lengthily rehearsed,
one after the other, their confident innocent pe-
titions.   The clear voices chirruped, but he shut
their words from his mind, as regardless as God.
Would they never finish?   To hear these dear
meaningless desiderations was too tender a torment.   He tried to think of other things—of anything—of the sea; of washing his hands and
putting on a clean collar; of the striped brown and

silver tie that he intended to wear to-morrow
(Joyce had never seen it); and what on earth are
we going to do to amuse these people after dinner?

". . . and Mother and Daddy and all friends
kind and dear; and let to-morrow be a nice day
for the Picnic . . ."

Poor little devils, he thought; they seem as far
away from me as if they were kittens or puppies.
People pretend that children are just human
beings of a smaller size, but I think they're something quite different. They live in a world with
only three dimensions, a physical world immersed
in the moment, a reasonable world, a world without that awful sorcery of a fourth measurement
that makes us ill at ease. What is it their world
lacks? Is it self-consciousness, is it beauty, is it
sex? (Three names for the same thing, perhaps.)
Little Sylvia with her full wet eyes, what torments
of desire she would arouse some day in some de-
luded stripling.

Strange world of theirs: a world that has no
awareness of good and evil; a world merely pretty,
whereas ours is beautiful. A world that knows
what it wants; whereas we are never quite
sure. . . .

He looked at them with amazement. Where
did they come from, how did they get there?

They were more genuine than himself, they would still be in this incredible life long after he had been shovelled out of it. How soon would they begin to see through the furious pettiness of parents? See that we do everything we punish them for attempting, that we torture them for our own weakness, set their teeth on edge for the taste of our own green grapes?

He tucked them in, gave each rounded hill of blanket a consoling pat, and left them. Joyce was standing in the passage. She had changed her clothes and was wearing a plain grey linen dress. He wanted to tell her that she was one of the unbelievably rare women who never have a pink strap of ribbon running loose across one shoulder. There must be *some* solution of that problem? A man would have abolished it long ago. But she's on her way to the bathroom, I suppose; it'll be more polite if I just stand aside and let her pass without saying anything. Besides, we can't talk here, right outside Ruth's door.

But she did not move. Evidently she had been watching his little scene with the children. In a flicker of the mind he wondered whether his part in it had looked creditable. He was afraid it had. For now, to her at any rate, he hankered to be known as the troubled imbecile he really was.

"And you wonder why I envy you," she said.

He didn't answer. He was busy reminding himself that that was what her eyes were like. It is only a few times that any man has the chance or the will to search the innermost bravery of other human faces. He had thought much about her eyes, had imagined the fine glory of telling them about themselves. Foreigners, he would call them; bright aliens not quite at home in the daily disasters of earth's commonplace. Foreigners, but he was on the pier waiting for them. They seemed to know that life is a precious thing and that we are always in danger of marring it. He imagined them as they would be if their shadow of questioning were skimmed away; if they were flooded with the light of complete surrender, of reckless trust. But how can these things be said? There is no code, he thought: so perhaps the wise presently abandon attempt to communicate. The gulf surrounds us all; only here and there on the horizon a reversed ensign shows where some stout spirit founders in silence. Or now and then, in the casual palaver of the day, slips out some fantastic phrase to show how man rises from clay to potter, can even applaud the nice malice of his own comedy.

He had got beyond the point where he could talk

to her in trivialities. He must say all or nothing.

"Lucky children," she said. "I wish *I* had someone to hear my prayers.—If I had, I might say some."

"I *didn't* hear them. I wasn't listening; I couldn't. Oh, Joyce, Joyce, there's so much I want to say, and your eyes keep interrupting me."

He thrilled a little at himself, and felt better. For he had his Moments: unforeseen felicities when he said the humorous and necessary word: and when his Moments came he could not help gloating over them. She gloated too, for she relished that innocent glee when he congratulated his own mind. When himself was his own guest of honour, and he stood genially at the front door.

So she smiled. What other woman could ever reward a lucky phrase with such magic of wistful applause?

"I apologize for them. They didn't mean to be rude."

She was so young and straight in her plain frock, so blessedly unconscious of herself. He thought of her fine strong body, the ungiven body that was so much her own, near him again after all the miracles of life that divide flesh from flesh and then bring it again within grasp; her sweet un-commanded beauty, irrelevant perhaps, yet so thrillingly a symbol of her essence. The noble body, poor blasphemed perfection, worshipped in the dead husks of statue and painting and yet so feared in its reality. He had to remind himself that it *was* irrelevant. How could any man with a full quota of biology help dream of mastering that cool, unroused detachment?

Ah, he had already had all of her that was imperishable: her dreams, her thoughts, her poor secret honesties. She had given him these, and nothing could spoil them. He had agreed with himself that his love was merely for her mind. (Distressing thought!) It was only the ridiculous need of keeping this passion to themselves that darkened and inflamed it. If it could be announced it would instantly become the purest thing on earth. It would be robbed of its sting. He imagined an engraved card:—

Mr. and Mrs. George Granville
have the honour to announce
the betrothal of Mr. Granville's mind
to that of Miss Joyce Clyde
Nothing Carnal

"Let me not to the marriage of true minds
Admit impediments."

But this would satisfy no one. Perhaps not even themselves. And people don't like things to be pure: it casts a rebuke on their own secrets.

"Joyce, let's make our announcement at this party."

"What announcement?" She looked startled.

"Why, that our minds are engaged."

Her hand, in his, tightened a little, reproachfully.

"George, before you go down. Who is this Mr. Martin?"

"I don't really know; some friend of Phyl's. I never saw him before. She says he's going to do a portrait of her. I think he's kidding her."

He turned toward the stairs and then called her back.

"Listen," he said softly. "When I say something, after dinner, about putting the car away, that's your cue. Slip away and come with me. I want to show you something."

XII

THE kitchen, that had been a core of fiery heat all day, was now more comfortable. Lizzie sat in an easy slouch, elbows on the oilcloth table cover, enjoying her own supper before attacking the great piles of dishes. The cleansed air, drifting through the open window, struck pleasantly on the moist glow of her body. There was a light tread on the back steps and the squeak of the screen door. The cook felt too deservedly slack to turn, but removed her mouth from the ear of corn just far enough to speak.

"Back early, ain't you?"

"Yeah. Brady's shofer was coming this way in their station wagon. Save me walking later on."

"Didn't expect you so soon, nice night like this."

"Well, Brady's bus was coming. Say, that fellow's got a nerve, all right."

Nounou tossed her hat on the shelf; ran her hands through her hair, sat down wearily in the other chair.

"Kids in bed?"

"Sure, before dinner. I'm glad you're back. You can give me a hand with the dishes."

"Where's all the folks?"

"On the porch."

Nounou got up, glanced cautiously through the pantry window, then took a cigarette from her bag and lit it. Lizzie, a native of Dark Harbour, reflected sombrely on the ways of metropolitan nursemaids.

"There's ice cream in the freezer if you want some."

"No, thanks. Brady's man blew me in the village. Gee, that boy's fresh."

Lizzie was a little annoyed at this repetition. It was a long time since any one had paid her the compliment of being fresh.

"It's the weather. Hot days and cool nights always makes trouble."

A brief silence. The kettle steamed softly on the range, Lizzie gnashed at her corncob, Nounou blew a gust of smoke and measured the stacks of dishes with a gloomy eye. Washing up was no part of her job, but she was somewhat in awe of the older woman; and the cook's dogged abstraction as she leaned over her food suggested that she had matter to impart.

"This place is certainly dead," Nounou grumbled. "Two miles to walk to the village, and a movie one night a week. Gosh, what a dump to spend summer in. Honest, Liz, I'm so tired workin', if I'd got that insurance o' mine paid up I'd quit a spell."

"Keeps you from thinkin,' don't it? If I had your job I wouldn't kick. Wear white cloes and lay out in the sun with them kids."

"You'd ought to get a place in the city. A good cook like you are could make big money."

"It ain't so dead round here as you might think. Say, you know that man was in the garden 'smorning, the one the children took such a shine to. Is he an old friend to the family?"

"Who?—the one that asked for a piece of cake? Never saw him before. I thought he acted kinda crazy."

"Well, they got him stayin' in the house. He must be someone they know pretty well, he calls 'em all to their first names. Say, I wish you'd seen 'em at supper, honest it was a sketch."

"Who all is there?"

"Mr. and Mrs. Brook, just usual sort o' people; and a dame they call Miss Clyde, dark and a bit serious-lookin'; and this Mr. Martin. Well, for the lovamike, when I go in to fix the table I

see smoke coming out from behind that screen in
the corner, I think something's afire. I run over
and there's Mr. Martin setting on the floor smoking on a cigarette. He looks at me sort of frightened, then he laughs and says not to tell anybody
because he's learnin' to make rings. He stands
around talkin' to me while I'm laying the table,
and then Mrs. G. comes in. He says to her 'Do
I have to go to bed right after dinner?' The
funny thing is he's got a cheerful kind of way about
him, you don't much mind what he does, he does
it so natural. Of course she knowed he was
jokin', she says he can set up as late as he likes.
He says it's nice to be able to do whatever you
want to and he asks me if we're going to have anything good for supper. Then he asks if he can ring
the gong. I always like to do that, he says. Mrs.
G. and me both busts out laughing. We laughed
and laughed like a couple of fools. I was trying
to remember what we was laughing at. I don'
know, we just screeched. He smiles too, kinda
surprised. There's something about him puts me
in mind of the way I used to find things comical
when I was a kid. I remember one day I got sent
home from school for laughing. It just struck
me funny to see the harbour out there and the

sunlight on the water and people going up and down the street talkin'."

Nounou tried to imagine what Lizzie looked like as a young girl, convulsed with mirth.

"They all comes in to eat. By and by, while I'm serving the consommay, he leans over and whispers to her—he's settin' at her right. No one else can hear, but I got it, I was right in back of 'em. When I'm in bed, he says, will you come and tuck me in? Well, I wish you could seen her, as red and rosy; she looks swell to-night anyhow in that silver layout o' hers. I never seen any one look prettier; I think that other dame, Mrs. Brook, was kinda sore at Mrs. G. for wearin' it."

Nounou put down her cigarette in amazement.

"You must've got them wrong," she said. "These ain't that kinda folks, you're crazy."

"You never know what kinda people people is till you live in the house with 'em. 'Course it don't mean nothing to me what-all stuff they pull. But listen what I'm telling you. This Mr. Martin is quiet, he don't talk an awful lot, but every once and a while he comes through with something that knocks 'em cold. Going to bed seems to be on his mind. Next thing he says, right out loud, 'It's nice being in bed, it gives you a chance to be alone.'

"I couldn't hear so much, bein' in an' out o' the room; an' the whole thing was on my shoulders anyways, because honest to God Mrs. G. was in some kind of a swound. I declare she didn't seem to know what-all was coming off. What with that Mr. Martin talking to me I forgot to put any bread at the places, and will you believe it she never took notice on it until Mrs. Brook piped up for some. When I pass Mrs. G. the peas she takes a ladlefull and holds it over her plate so long I didn't know what to do. Oh, of course, they all talk along smart and chirpy, the way folks does at a dinner party, pretend to kid each other an' all, but I can see it don't mean nothing. Mrs. Brook has some line she thinks a lot of, she springs it on Miss Clyde, I reckon you're wedded to your art she says, throwing it at her pretty vicious. It was bad for Mrs. Brook, I'll admit, setting between Mr. Martin and Mr. G. Because Mr. G. don't make up to her none, he's talking to the Clyde girl all the time; and Mr. Martin don't buzz her none neither. She sings out how much she does love children and Mr. Martin says But do they love you? A good piece of the time she has to talk to her husband, across the table, and you know that makes any woman sore at a party. Once and a while Mrs. G. comes to life

and says something about what a good time we'll
have to the Picnic; this Martin says Yes, he
hankers to see Mr. Granville climb a tree. Mr. G.
wants to know what he'll be climbing trees for.
'Why,' says Mr. Martin, 'I heard her say you'd
be up a tree if that check didn't come in to-day.'
Then Mr. Martin says he likes the way Mr. G.
and Miss Clyde looks at each other, as though they
had secrets together. He's got an attractive
way to him, but it seems like he says whatever
comes into his head. What-all way is that to
behave?"

Lizzie had looked forward to telling Nounou
about the dinner. Now she felt with a keen dis-
appointment that it was impossible to describe it
adequately. Besides, what she had intended to
say would perhaps sound too silly. Mr. Martin
looks like some old lover of Mrs. G's, she thought,
that's turned up unexpected. He's kinda forgotten about her, put her outa his life. But she's
mad about him, all her heart's old passion is re-
vived. Better not say too much about these
things to Nounou anyhow; she might let Brady's
man go too far.

"Come on, kid," she said, getting up from the
table. "Give me a hand with this stuff. I gotta
get this kitchen clean, the madam will be coming

in here afterwhile to cut sandwiches. We get this finished, we can hit the hay."

Nounou smiled a little as she took the dish-towel.

"I'll help you clean up," she said. "Then I'm going to slip out a while longer."

XIII

NOW it was dusk: dusk that takes away the sins of the world. Under that soft cone of shadow, wagged like a dunce cap among the stars, are folly and glamour and despair; but no sin. The day was going back to the pure darkness where all things began; to the nothing from which it had come; to the unconsciousness that had surrounded it. The long, long day had orbed itself to a whole. Its plot and scheme were perfect; its crises and suspenses artfully ordered; now darkness framed it and memory gave it grace. Tented over by upward and downward light, mocked by tinsel colours and impossible desires, another cunning microcosm was complete.

"I like your orchestra," said Joyce. They were all sitting on the veranda steps. From the garden and the dunes beyond came the rattling tremolo of summer insect choirs.

No one spoke for a moment. Phyllis was enjoying a relaxation after the effort of the dinner table. It was no longer necessary to think, every instant, of something to say. Darkness takes the

place of conversation. It replies to everything.
Like fluid privacy the shadow rose and flowed
restfully about them; faces were exempt from scrutiny; eyes, those timid escapers from question,
could look abroad at ease. Reprieved from angers
and anxieties, the mind yearned to come home
under the roof of its little safe identity. It
had not forgotten the distractions that make
life hard: quarrels, the income tax, unanswered
letters, toothache: but these hung for a moment,
merely a pretty sparkle of fireflies. I feel as
though I were really Me, Phyllis thought. I wish
there were someone to hold my hand.

I wonder if I *do* like it? Joyce thought as soon
as she heard her own voice.

Come home, come home to yourself, cried the
incessant voice of darkness. The soulless musi-
cians of earth fiddled with horrid ironic gusto.
Nothing is true but desire, they wailed and
wheedled. Now they were fierce piccolo and pi-
broch; now they had the itinerant rhythm of
bawdy limericks.

Special intensity of silence seemed to emanate
from Ben and Ruth, who sat close together on the
top step. In the general pause theirs was like a
hard core: it was not true silence but only repressed speech. The smell of Ben's cigar floated

among the group like an argument. It had a sensible, civilized, matter-of-fact, downtown fragrance. It seemed to suggest that someone—even the crickets, perhaps—should put down a proposition in black and white. Joyce had a feeling that Ben and Ruth were waiting for any one to say anything; and that when it was said they would jointly subject it to careful businesslike scrutiny. Contents noted, and in reply would say——

"Orchestra?" repeated Ben, in a puzzled voice.

"The crickets." (She tried not to make it sound like an explanation.) "I'd forgotten that nights on the Island were like this."

Martin was sitting just below her. He had been playing with the pebbles on the path, picking them up and dropping them. He turned and looked up at her.

"Like what?" he asked.

She had the same sensation of disbelief she had felt at the dinner table. One must be strangely innocent or strangely reckless to ask questions like that. George's face shone in the flare of a match: he looked emptily solemn and pensive as men always do while lighting a pipe. Joyce felt almost as though there were a kind of conspiracy against her to make her take the lead in talking.

"They fiddle away as though it was the most

important night that ever happened," she said, a little nervously. "As though they think it's a First Night and the reviewers are here from the newspapers."

"It *is* the most important night that ever happened," said Phyllis slowly. "It's *now*." There was a queer frightened tremble in her voice.

"There'll be a moon a little later," said George. He said it rather as though this would be creditable to him, as host.

"No, George, don't let there be a moon. Not everything at once, it's too much."

Something in George's outline showed that he thought Phyllis was merely chaffing him; but Joyce was more clairvoyant. For the first time she became aware of some reality in Phyllis: saw that she was more than just George's wife. There was in her some buried treasure that no one had ever taken the trouble to hunt for. Why, she's lovely, Joyce thought. In a sudden impulse she wanted to take Phyllis's hand; her own fluttered liftingly in her lap; she restrained it, for she felt that she would want to kiss George before very long and it didn't seem quite square to be in love with a man and his wife simultaneously. It would be extravagant, she supposed sadly.

"We don't need a moon," she said, "with Mrs. Granville wearing that lovely silver dress."

"It makes me feel as though we ought to do something special," said Martin.

"We can have a game of Truth," suggested George.

No one showed much enthusiasm except Martin, who wanted to know how it was played.

"Everyone must tell some thought he has had but didn't say."

Ben and Ruth felt more certain than ever that the evening was going to be a failure.

"A thought you've had *ever?*" asked Martin.

"No, this evening."

"You suggested it, George; you can go first," said Ruth.

"Ruth evidently believes that unspoken thoughts are always terrible."

"They can't be much more terrible than some of the things that were said at dinner," Ruth retorted.

"In this game you don't get to the really interesting stuff until after several rounds, when people get warmed up. I'll begin with a very small one. I was thinking that I mustn't forget to put away the car.—Now Ruth, what's yours?"

"That Miss Clyde probably has a very becoming bathing suit."

"I was thinking I heard one of the children calling," said Phyllis. "But it wasn't, it was only a singing in my nose."

"What a funny nose," said Martin.

"Don't you know how something seems to get caught in your nostril and makes a kind of singing when you breathe?"

Ben had had time to make a careful choice of the least damning of his meditations. "I was thinking that the crickets don't really sound like an orchestra. They're more like adding machines."

"Why, that's true," George exclaimed. "They have just that even, monotonous, cranking sound. Adding up some impossible and monstrous total. Counting the stars, maybe."

"I hope you won't think my thought is rude," said Joyce. "It struck me that if it weren't for Mr. Brook's cigar I'd be convinced this is all a dream.—I don't mean it isn't a nice cigar, just that it smells so worldly."

"Well, our secret thoughts all seem fairly innocent. But we haven't heard yours yet, Mr. Martin."

"I don't think this is a very interesting game," said Martin.

George insisted. "Come, the guest of honour can't escape as easily as that. Out with it!"

"Do I have to?" Martin appealed to Phyllis. She came out of her reverie, aware that even darkness is inadequate as a sedative. The threads of relationship among them all had tightened.

"I know what Mr. Martin's trouble is," said Ruth. "He says everything he thinks, so naturally he has nothing left."

"Why, that's just it," Martin said. "How did you know? What would be the good of thinking things and not saying them?"

"You're not playing fair," George objected. "No one would be crazy enough to say everything. Besides, there wouldn't be time."

Martin was stubbornly silent.

"I agree with Mr. Martin," Phyllis said. "It's not a very cheerful game. If we didn't say our thoughts we must have had some good reason for keeping them silent. Besides, I must speak to Lizzie about breakfast."

"I'll take the car to the stable."

"Can I go with you?" Martin asked.

George had still cherished a forlorn hope that the world was large enough for him and Joyce to have a few moments alone. For several days the stable had been sanctified in his anticipation.

In the hayloft above the old disused stalls there was a big doorway that opened toward the sea. That mustily fragrant place was his favourite retreat when solitude seemed urgent. There, he had thought, he and Joyce could talk. He had even put an old steamer rug on the hay so they might sit more comfortably. There would be moonlight over the water. . . .

"Is it the same stable where we used to play as kids?" cried Ruth. "Oh, let's all go. I want to see it again. Why, that old haymow was the first place Ben ever kissed me."

"What did he do that for?" said Martin.

"Perhaps he'll do it again," said George bitterly. It was just like Ruth to ruin the stable for him.

"Well, I don't want to spoil any one else's plans," said Ben.

"We could play hide-and-seek in the hay," Martin suggested.

Now they were all piling into the car, to ride round the house to the stable. This was of a piece with the absurdity of everything else, George thought. People were always driving up in crowds to visit his secrets. Like sight-seeing busses loaded with excursionists. The world loves to trample over your private ecstasies and leave them littered with scraps of paper and banana peel. And this fellow Martin, with his cool mockery, was beginning to get on his nerves.

The engine leapt into life with the same eager alacrity as if they had been starting off for a long drive. Yes, the human objective means nothing to the routine of Nature. She looses her lightning indifferently, whether between the sooty termini of a spark plug or from charged cloud to earth. She squanders as much energy in a meadow of hallooing crickets as in a human spirit tormented by conflicting passions.

They made the circuit of the house. Down the drive from the front door to the main road, along the side of the house, then up the back lane by the kitchen and the circular bed of cannas. Only a hundred yards, but it seemed interminable because it was futile and meaningless. Something had gone wrong in his time sense. As the car passed the kitchen window he could see Phyllis talking to Lizzie, holding up a loaf of bread as she spoke. At the same moment Ruth was saying something about the moon coming up. His mind went off in a long curve. He felt a gush of anger at Phyllis because she had been so unaware of his feeling for Joyce. If she had been spiteful, or jealous, or suspicious, how much easier it would

have been. Her pettiness would have driven him
and Joyce blissfully into each other's arms, without the faintest sense of remorse. But this
strangely detached Phyllis who seemed to move
in a dream, instead of the familiar Phyllis of
tempers and reproaches, was a different problem.
Even sin, he thought furiously, is to be made as
difficult as possible for me. And I had always
imagined it would be so easy. Will God ever
forgive me if I don't commit the sins I was intended to? God will get no praise from me, He's
packed the house with a claque of crickets to put
the show over. Through the window Phyllis's
golden head shone in a haze of lamplight. As
always, when angry at her he loved her most.
When you love a woman, why make her life
miserable by marrying her? Marriage demands
too much. . . .

From this speculation he came back to find
Ruth just finishing her sentence, the car still op-
posite the window, the loaf of bread still lifted in
Phyllis's hand. It occurred to him that this
evening was damnably like the slowed motion-
pictures in which the stream of life is retarded into
its component gestures. Now he was to have the
embarrassment of witnessing the actual rhythm
of living, the sluggish pattern that underlies gay

human ritual, the grave airy dancing of creation treading softly its dark measure to unheard, undreamed music. The smallest alteration in the mind's pace changes everything, as some trifling misprint turns a commonplace newspaper headline into obscenity.

They drove into the stable.

"I miss the nice old horsey smell," said Ruth. "Too bad, it's only a garage now."

"Which was it you wanted to revive, the horsey smell or the embraces of Ben?" said George. "The loft hasn't changed much, I think."

He snapped on the light. While the others climbed the narrow little stair behind the old feed bins he filled the radiator with water and poured oil into the crank case. Morosely he heard their words overhead.

"Someone's left a blanket up here."

"Look, the bay's all full of moonlight. I didn't remember it was like that."

"We were children then, we didn't know about the moon. We had to go to bed too early."

"The old swing's gone." (This was Mr. Martin's voice.)

"Why . . . how did you know? Yes, that's where it was, that beam. . . ."

I thought that lunatic had been here before,

George said to himself. He seems to know his way about.

He started the motor again. He thought he had noticed a faint roughness in its turning. He listened attentively, marvelling at the strong, hurrying fidelity of those airy explosions. I know why this car has kept her youth, he thought. She hasn't had any proper care, but she's been loved. A soft throbby purring, with a sweet quavering rhythm; the sound of sliding, of revolving, of vapour evenly expelled. It was a consoling, normal kind of sound; complete in itself; it shut out the voices upstairs. A touch on the throttle and it rose to a growl of unused power, a shout of fierce unquestioning assent, not much different from defiance. The old barn rang. It was as if an officer of some colonial regiment called on his legions for a fatal exploit, and heard in their answering yell a voice of savagery that might turn against himself.

He switched the key; the sound slid off into a soft conclusive sigh. There was an almost human breath of frustration in it. He closed the hood, his mind too vague for thinking, and saw Joyce standing there.

"I thought Mr. and Mrs. Brook would like a moment of privacy," she whispered.

He had her in his arms. On her soft lips was all
the bittersweet of their long separation, of their
mirth together, of their absurd and precious passion, denied by men and ratified by crickets. It
was the perfect embrace of those who are no
longer children, who can sweeten the impossible by
mocking it a little. The tingling triumph of
social farce, undreamed by poor candid Nature
—the first illicit kiss!

"I suppose," she said tremulously, "that this
really is what they call a Guilty Passion."

"My dear, my dear. What a queer world,
where one has to apologize for loving people."

As though down a long avenue of distance he
saw her in the perspective of her life: an exquisite
gallant figure going about her brave concerns:
so small and resolute in her single struggle with
the world, and coming to his arms at last. He
knew then that poets have not lied; that fairy
tales are true; that life is hunger, and for every
emptiness caters its own just food. Her mind
that he had loved was tangled up with a body.
Chastity was probably a much overrated virtue.
For her sake, if she desired it, he was willing to
make the heroic effort which is necessary to yield
to temptation.

He held her close, in silence. Austere resolu-

tions slipped away like sand in an hour glass.
For an instant his only thought was a silly satisfaction that she must reach so far upward to meet
his lips. His mind taunted him for thinking
this.

"Dear fool, dear damned fool," he said. "Yes,
you're just as you should be: lips cool and eyelids
warm. And as soft as I always imagined. Oh, it's
not fair that any one should be so soft. Joyce, do
you know why I had to have you here? It's just
a year . . . you remember?"

"Yes. The day you were looking out of the
window. How long it seems."

"We begin to feel like a nice old unmarried
couple."

She laughed, her rare broken laugh.

"Oh, George, then it *is* really you. The Fourth
you, I mean. I couldn't quite believe it."

Voices came down from the loft. First it was
Martin:

. . . "That's what I like about her. She
looks as if she's happy inside."

Then Ruth, with a scornful snicker:

"Happy? I dare say. Did you see the way she
looked at George at the dinner table? That kind
of woman's always happy with someone else's
husband."

There was an inaudible murmur, then Ben's voice:

"It's a form of nervousness."

Joyce drew back from his arms. Her eyes were dark with horror.

"Oh . . ." she said with a sob. "Why are people so . . . so *inadequate*."

Ruth's little sneer, falling on them like a crystal spirt of poison, burned George's bare heart.

"Joyce, dear Joyce . . ." He put his hands on her shoulders. "I must tell you, I must. I've waited so long. Oh, it's so long since I've done anything I want to, I've forgotten how. Joyce, you don't know how I needed you. I was hungry, I was a beggar, you fed me with laughter and taught me how to suffer. You taught me how to love, yes, everything I love I love a thousand times better because I know you. God help me, I love even Phyllis better because of you. . . ."

With a gesture of pathos and despair she buried her face in his coat. They heard the others beginning to descend. To postpone for a few moments the necessity of speech, he turned wildly to the car and again started the engine. As Ruth appeared at the foot of the stairs, her mouth opening to say something, he speeded the motor to a roar.

"Oh, George," piped Ruth as they were walking back to the house. "I've left my scarf. I must have dropped it in the loft. Ben'll get it. Have you locked the barn?"

"No, we don't lock anything around here."

"You laugh at locksmiths," said Joyce.

"I'll go," George said. "I can find it easier than Ben. There's a flashlight in the car."

He walked back to the stable. A lemonade-coloured moon was swimming above the maple tree. He did not bother to get the torch but slipped up the stair, moving noiselessly on rubber soles. The scarf was lying just at the top, where the steps emerged into the old harness room. He was about to glance into the hayloft, to satisfy his sentimental vision of how it would have looked to him and Joyce, a cavern of country fragrance, a musk of dead summers still banked there in pourried mounds. He was halted, with a catch of breath, by murmuring voices. He peered round the doorpost. A slope of powdery moon-light carved a pale alley through the heavy shadow. On his rug, spread toward the open window, sat Nounou and Brady's man, ardently enlaced.

The whispering pair, engrossed in rudimentary endearment, were oblivious of all else. It amused him to reflect that they must have been hiding anxiously somewhere in the loft while the visitors palavered near them. A single cricket, embalmed in the hay, chirped sweet airy prosits— solitary lutanist (or prothalamist) of the occasion. George stood smitten by the vulgar irony. There was cruel farce and distemper in finding his own dear torment parodied in these terms of yokel dalliance. The parable was only too plain. This back-yard amour was as rich in Nature's eyes as the kingliest smoke-room story of the Old Testament. Nature, genial procuress, who impartially honours the breach and the observance.

With the crude humour of the small boy, never quite buried in any man, he emitted a loud groaning wail of mimic anguish. He thrilled with malicious mirth to see the horrified swains leap up in panic. He tiptoed stealthily away, leaving them aghast.

This has got to end, he said to himself.

G

XIV

IF THERE were only one moonshiny night in
each century, men would never be done talking of it. Old lying books would be consulted;
in padded club chairs grizzled gentry whose grand-
fathers had witnessed it would prate of that milky
pervasion that once diluted the unmixed absolute
of night. And those who had no vested gossip
in the matter would proclaim it unlikely to recur,
or impossible to have happened.

Mr. and Mrs. Brook and Martin had gone on
toward the veranda. Joyce lingered where the
edge of the house's shadow was a black frontier
on the grass. The lawn was a lake of pallor.
Under the aquamarine sky, glazed like the curly
inmost of a shell, earth was not white or glittering,
but a soft wash of argentine grey. There was
light enough to see how invisible the world truly
is The pure unpurposeful glamour poured like
dissolving spirit on the dull fogged obscure of
ordinary evening: the cheap veneers of shadow
peeled away, true darkness was perceivable: the
dark that threads like marrow in the bones of

things: the dark in which light is only an accidental tremble. Where trees and shrubs glowed in foamy tissue, hung chinks and tinctures of appeasing nothing. This was abyss unqualified, darkness neat.

She was drowned at the bottom of this ocean of transparency. She felt as people look under water, pressed out of shape, refracted, blurred by the pressure of an enormous depth of love. In such clean light a thought, a memory, a desire, could put on shape and living, stare down the cautious masks of habit. The trustiest senses could play traitor inside this bubble of pearly lustre; the hottest bonfires of mirth would be only a flicker in this dim stainless peace. Better to go indoors, join the polite vaudeville of evasion, escape the unbearable reality of this enchanted . . .

"Here you are!" said a voice. "Thank goodness. I want to ask you things. You're different."

It was Martin.

"What's the matter with all these people?" he exclaimed. "Why can't they have fun? Why do they keep on telling me they love me? I don't want to be loved. You can't be happy when you're being loved all the time. It's a nuisance.

I want to build castles in the sand and play croquet and draw pictures. I want to go to bed
and get a good sleep for the Picnic; and that lady
wants me to kiss her. I did it once; isn't that
enough?"

Here was a merriment: to expect her, at this
particular junction of here and now, to join his
deprecations.

"Quite enough," she said. "But it depends on
the person. She may not think so."

"It's Mrs. Phyllis. I asked her if she was ready
for me to go to bed, and she said I mustn't say
such things. What's the matter with her? I
think she's angry. Everybody seems angry. Why
is it?"

Her pulses were applauding her private thought:
If Phyllis loves *him*, I can love George.

"And I saw Bunny in the garden. She says
you're the only one who can help me because you
almost understand."

"Bunny! Bunny who? What do you
mean? . . ."

He must be mad. Yet it seemed an intelligible
kind of madness: some unrecognized but urgent
meaning sang inside it like a sweet old tune. In
the misty moonlight she saw the great wheel of
Time spinning so fast that its dazzling spokes

seemed to shift and rotate backward. But her mind still intoned its own jubilee: If Phyllis loves *him*, I can love George. It's all right for me to love George. Be ye lift up, ye everlasting doors!

"Bunny Richmond, of course. She's playing some kind of hide-and-seek round here. It's not fair."

"It *is* fair!" cried Bunny passionately. He could hear her calling to him from somewhere just round the corner of the path. "Oh, Martin, Martin, can't you see? I can't *tell* you, you've got to find out for yourself."

Bunny had cried out so eagerly that even Joyce almost heard her. She turned to look.

"What was that, someone whispering?"

"It's only Bunny," he said impatiently. "She's playing tricks on me. She wants me to go away."

Joyce had stepped out of the shadow, and now Martin partly saw.

"Why, I know who you are. Why . . . why, of course. They called you Miss Clyde, that fooled me. You're not Miss Anybody, you're Joyce . . . the one who gave me the mouse. *You* don't love me too, do you? People only love you when they want you to do things."

Bunny kept calling him, but he closed his ears to her.

"No, I don't love you," she said slowly. "I love George."

But she had to look at him again to be sure. He was very beautiful and perplexed. Perhaps she loved everybody. For an instant she thought he *was* George; she could see now that there was a faint resemblance between them. Then she noticed that George was there too. He had come along the path from the stable. His face was sharpened with resolve. He paid no attention to Martin, but spoke directly to her.

"Here's your scarf," he said, almost roughly, holding it out. Then he remembered it was not hers, and thrust it in his pocket. He made an uncertain step toward her.

"Oh, we can't go on like this," he said harshly. "This has got to . . ." He made a queer awkward gesture with his arms. She went to them.

"How funny you are," observed Martin from the shadow. "First you want to push her away and then you hug her."

Apparently George did not hear him.

"Why did you wake me?" he was asking her.

"Why couldn't I go on sleepwalking through life? If I had never known you, how much anguish I'd have missed. Oh, my poor dear."

"You mustn't talk to her like that," said Martin. "This is Joyce, she thinks once is enough. She isn't like Phyllis."

"Go away, Martin," called Bunny. "It's no use now."

George held her fiercely. His voice trembled on broken words of tenderness. His bewildered mind craved the ease of words, a little peace, a little resting time. Must this glory of desire be carried for ever secret in his heart?

"You'll hurt her," said Martin angrily.

This they had stumbled on, George's heart cried to him. It was none of their seeking. She belongs to who can understand her, insisted the sweet sophistries of blood. Joyce leaned up to him, the dear backward curve of woman yearning to the face of her dream.

"Don't you know me?" Martin appealed to her. "You gave me the mouse yesterday."

He was unheeded. They did not even know he was there.

"You're doing it too," he said to her bitterly, and went away.

"George, when did I give you a mouse?"

"A mouse? What are you talking about? You're going to give me something much better than a mouse. Do you know what I said to you once in a dream? I said, the worst of my love for you is that it's so carnal."

Her eyes met his, troubled but steady.

"And do you know what you answered?"

"No," she said pitifully. "Oh, George, George, I don't know about these things."

"You said, 'Perhaps that's what I like about it.'"

She clung to him in a kind of terror.

"I don't know whether I said that. George . . . don't let's be like other people. Does it *matter?*"

They stood together and the crickets shouted, rattled tiny feet of approval on the floor of the dunes like a gallery of young Shelleys. The whole night was one immense rhythm; up the gully from the beach came a slow vibration of surf. She was weak with the question in her blood, her knees felt empty. Perhaps that's where your morality is kept, in the knees, she thought. She slipped her arms under his coat, round the hard strong case of his ribs, to keep from tottering. The tobacco smell of his lapel was infinitely precious and pathetic.

"How do I know what matters?" he whispered. "We can wait and see. If it's important, the time will come. But I want you to know, my love for you is complete. It wants everything. Can't you hear the whole world singing it? Everything, everything, everything."

"I don't like the crickets. They're trying to get us into trouble."

Everything is so queer this evening, she thought. How did all this happen? I'm frightened.

"We've always been different from other people," she said. "We're absurd and pitiful and impossible. Don't let's spoil it, let's just be *us*."

His arms held her more gently. For love is beyond mere desire: it is utter tenderness and pity. Sing, world, sing: here are your children caught in the chorus of that old, old music; here are Food and Hunger that meet only to cancel and expire. Here, cries Nature in her deepest diapason, here are my bread and wine. Too great to be accused of blasphemy, she shames not to borrow the words of man's noblest fancy. Take, eat, she cries to the famished. This is my body which is given for you. Do this in remembrance of me. And her children, conscious of lowly birth, can rise to denials her old easy breast never dreamed.

G*

"George," said Joyce quickly, "is any one watching . . . listening to us? I've had the strangest feeling. As though someone was trying to tell me something, calling me."

"A singing in your nose, perhaps."

"No, but really."

"I've been trying to tell you something."

"Where did Mr. Martin go? Wasn't he there?"

"I didn't see him."

They turned toward the house. Its dark shadow hung over them, clear, impalpable, black as charcoal. They felt purified by mutual confession and charity.

"I think it was the house listening to us," she said. "Why am I so happy?"

He knew that he loved her. It was not lust, for though he desired her and a thousand times had had her in his heart, yet he shrank from possession, fearing it might satiate this passion that was so dear. So it was a fool's love: perhaps a coward's, since to be taken is every woman's need. But who shall say? Life is a foreign language: all men mispronounce it.

He loved her, for he saw the spirit of life in her. He loved her as a dream, as something he himself had created, as someone who had helped to create part of him. He loved her because it was secret, hopeless, impossible. He had loved her because he could not have her: and now she was here for his arms. The Dipper and the wind in the pine trees said, Poor fool, if you want her, take her. The black flap in the sky, where the starry pinning has fallen out (it opens into the law of gravity) said, It concerns only yourselves, no one will know. The tide and the whistling sand dunes said, She's yours already.

From the sleeping porch over their heads he heard one of the children cough.

"George," she whispered, "I'll do whatever you tell me."

He turned to her. "I'd like to see *any one* laugh at locksmiths."

XV

THEY were entrenched in a little fortress of light. The tall silk-shaded lamp made the living hall an orange glow, an argument against silver chaos veined with brute nothing. The clock, the clock, the clock, measured itself against the infidel crickets. Phyllis, in a corner of the big sofa, was in the centre of that protecting glitter. She was panoplied in light: it poured upon the curve of her nape, sparkled in the bronze crisp of her hair, brimmed over the soft bend of her neck and ran deep down into the valley of her bosom. It rippled in scarps and crumples of her shining dress, struck in through the gauzy chiffon, lay in flakes on the underskirt, gilded the long slope of her stockings like the colour of dawn on snow. She could feel it, warm and defiant, wrapping her close, holding her together. Even her bright body, in such fragile garb, was hardly dark.

But the reality was still that pale emptiness outside. Where she sat she could see, beyond the dining room and the high rectangle of French windows, a pure shimmer of white night. Down

the broad open well of the stair the same tender
void came drifting, floating, sinking. Summer
night cannot be shut out: it is heavier than thin
lamp-shine, it spreads along the floor, gathers beneath chairs, crowds up behind pictures, makes
treacherous friendship with the gallant little red-
headed bulbs.

She felt soft and ill. She felt her pliant body
settling deeper into the thick cushion, her hands
weighing inert upon her lap. She wished Ben and
Ruth could be restful for a moment. Ruth was
flitting about, looking at the furniture; Ben,
though sitting quietly, kept blowing cigar smoke
in a kind of rhythmical indignation. She could
see his mind toiling, so plainly that she would not
have been surprised to read words written in his
spouts of smoke, as in the balloon issuing from the
mouth of a comic drawing. If Mr. Martin would
only say something. He had just come in from
the garden, without a word, and sat expectantly at
the foot of the stairs. He was outside the circle
of light, she could not see him clearly, but he
seemed to be looking at her with inquiry or reproach. For being such a dull hostess, probably.

But speech was impossible. Now, with eyes
widened by terror and yearning, she was almost
aware of the sleepy world that lies beneath the

mind's restless flit: the slow cruel world, without conscience, that the artist never quite forgets. In the glare of the lamp the room burned with subordinate life: the grainy wood of the furniture, the nap of the rug, the weave of the sofa, were fibred with obstinate essence. Being was in them as in her, went on and on. It seemed as though one sudden push, if it could be made, might break through the fog of daily bickerings and foresights and adjustments, into that radiant untroubled calm. But conscious life tends to take the level of the lowest present: with Ruth and Ben and even the house itself steadfast against her, how could she speak out? The darkness that, outdoors, had been sweet privacy, was here obverted into secrecy: secrecy lay under the chairs, behind the doors, between the ticks of the clock. She had settled this room, only a few hours before, with so much care—dusting, arranging; everything in its accustomed pose. Now it was too strong for her, and every pattern in it ran with shouts of taunting laughter. . . . It was just like George to linger in the garden, leaving her alone to "entertain" these guests.

Then she was aware that someone had spoken. She had not caught the words, but the sound poised in her mind. It was a pleasant sound, it must have been Mr. Martin. Perhaps she would go through all the rest of her life without knowing what he had said. Yet it might have been a cry for help. You never know, she thought, when people may leave off pretending and lay their heads on your breast. What a silly way to put it: lay their head—his head—on your breasts; because you have only one head and two breasts. Perhaps that's why the insects make such an uproar, shrilling sour grapes. They're jealous because they're not mammals. . . .

"He went back to the stable to get my scarf."

"I hope they won't catch cold," said Phyllis. "It's so much cooler to-night."

"You oughtn't to kiss people when you have a cold," said Martin.

This, Phyllis supposed, was a little reckless aside for her alone. She felt a bright seed of anger in her; it was sprouting, climbing up the trellis of her nerves. She had a fine fertility for anger; her mind was shallow soil as its bottom had never been spaded: such seeds could not root deeply and slowly, so they shot upward in brilliant quick-withering flower. The rising warmth medicined her empty sickness. He was cruel, but she loved him for it and could have prostrated herself at his feet. What right had he to be so untouched, so happy and certain and sure? His mind was one, not broken up into competing yearnings.

"Competition is the life of trade," she said.

Looking up, she wondered if she had said something accidentally witty From the other side of the room Ruth was regarding her strangely. Beyond Ruth, black against the blanched evening, were George and Joyce on the veranda steps. . . . Oh, so that was what Martin had meant?

Ben's face was so perplexed and bored, she took pity on him.

"What would you people like to do? Play cards? We can't dance, there isn't any music."

Ruth was quite content not to dance; she suspected she would have had to take Ben as a partner. "Ben's favourite game is Twenty Questions," she said.

"Gracious, I haven't played that in ages. It'll be rather fun. Here come the others, let's do it."

George seemed almost like a stranger, Phyllis thought. She had an impish desire to ask to be introduced. It amused her to think that any one should want to kiss him.

"What a gorgeous night." He spoke loudly, rather as if someone might contradict. "Here's your scarf," he added, almost roughly, holding it out to Joyce. Then he remembered, and gave it to Ruth.

"How funny you are," said Martin. "You made the same mistake again."

"Thank you so much," Ruth said. "I'm sorry you had such a long hunt for it."

Joyce crossed the room in silence. Ruth's eyes followed her, and it was in Ruth's face that Phyllis first saw Joyce was beautiful. She brought some of the moonlight with her. No man can ever admire a woman's loveliness as justly as another woman, for he rarely understands how her fluctuating charm depends on the hazard of the instant. Something had happened to make Joyce beautiful, and Phyllis was surprised by an immense compassion. This creature too was lonely, had her bewildered tumult in the blood, was defenceless and doomed. Ruth's watchful eyes, unseen by Joyce, were asking her whether she had anything to say for herself, anything that could be used against her. And Ruth (Phyllis could see) was as outraged by Joyce mute as she would have been at anything she said.

Joyce was helpless: helpless, because she was happy; helpless, for she had brought no words with her. She had brought only moonlight and it was

declared contraband.   In the instant that the girl
hesitated in the choice of a seat, Phyllis knew that
she could have loved her, they could have come together in a miracle of understanding, but Ruth had
made it impossible.   Ruth, the comely fidget, who
would never know the stroke of any grievance
greater than her own jealous mischiefs.   What
could Ruth know of the great purifying passions,
who had always forestalled them by yielding to the
pettiest?   The seedling anger in Phyllis's heart,
sensitively questing an object, swayed outward as
a young vine leans toward sun.   She would not
think of the Brooks again as Ben and Ruth.   They
were Ruth and Ben.   She knew now why Ben
peeped so warily from behind a rampart of seden-
tary filing cabinets.   His soul lurked behind the
greatest of hiding places, a huge office building.

With a swift impulse she reached out, beckoning
to a place beside her on the sofa.   Joyce's hand
was cold and seemed surprised.   The two hands,
like casual acquaintances meeting by accident,
lingered together wondering how to escape politely.
Phyllis realized it was not a success.   She leaned
forward to speak brightly to George, so that her
fingers might seem to slip free unawares.

"We're going to play Twenty Questions."

"Fine!" said George.   This, he thought, would

prevent general conversation, the one thing most to be feared.

"Ben, you go out," Phyllis suggested. Ben deserved some amusement, he had been rather patient in the middle of this silent turmoil.

"Let Ruth," said Ben. "She's clever at guessing things."

"No, Ben, you," Ruth said definitely. She was having too good a time guessing as she was.

From the sofa Joyce could see into the little dark sitting room—*her* room: her only retreat. It drew her strongly. The frame of the window opened into moonlight and a queer twist of shadows. If only she could go in there, get away. Here, under the lamp, everything was too full of dangerous artifice. The light held everything together tightly, in a bursting tension. No one could say anything for fear it, would have a double meaning. One meaning at a time was burden enough.

Was there anything queer about that little room? Mr. Martin, sitting at the bottom of the stairs, was close to the door: he was looking there too. In the back of her mind she remembered that she had started to say something to him in the garden; or he to her, she was not certain which; but something had been left unfinished. George was watching her, watching her; she could feel it, and needed to escape into herself. How could she escape? He knew all about her now, she found him round the remotest corners of her mind. No, no, there were lovely things about her that he did not guess. If she could be alone for a few minutes she could find out what they were. . . . So this was love, this dreadful weakness. It ought to be so easy; free and easy, that gay old phrase; and the taut web of human nerves frustrated it. Beside her, in a glitter of light, Phyllis shone mysteriously. The touch of that warm hand had shocked Joyce. She knew now that they could never be at peace together.

"I'll go," she said suddenly.

Phyllis, still leaning forward, was listening.

"Was that one of the children?"

As Joyce rose, getting up with difficulty from the deep settee, Martin closed the sitting-room door with a quick push. Why did he do that? Now it would seem rude to go in there. George, whose ear was cocked toward upstairs, looked angrily at him.

"I didn't hear anything. You've got the children on the brain, Phyl."

"I'll go on the veranda while you think of something," Joyce said.

It was amusing to see how eagerly they all turned to the old almost forgotten pastime. She heard them mumbling together while they concerted their choice. They were like savages at a campfire, rehearsing some cheerful ceremonial to dispel sorcery. The bare mahogany of the dining table was glossed with panels of dim colour. This led her eyes upward to the red and blue window. It reminded her distantly of some poem, some perfect enchantment that mocked the poor futility of her own obsession. That most magic outcry of unreflecting love, from the most wretched of lovers: the eternal collision between life as dreamed and life as encountered.

There was a burst of laughter.

"She'll never guess that," she heard Ruth saying.

"All ready," George called.

"There are five of us, you can go round four times. You must ask questions that can be answered by Yes or No."

She began in the traditional way.

"Is it animal?"

"No," said Ruth.

"Is it vegetable?"

"Yes," said Phyllis.

"Is it in this room?"

"Yes," said Ben.

The part of her that was asking questions seemed separate from her racing undertow of feeling. She was the frightened child who was shy about games because she was always playing and watching simultaneously. What should she ask? It was vegetable and in the room She had a preposterous eagerness to say something wildly absurd, she was weary of telling lies. If it had been Animal, she might have said "Is it George's love for me?" Their faces would have been comic. But it was Vegetable. . . . My vegetable love shall grow Vaster than empires and more slow . . . but if I quote that it will have to be explained. Why do poems insist on coming into the mind at instants of trouble?

"Is it Mr. Brook's cigar?"

"No," said George.

"Is it associated with some person in this room?"

"Yes," said Martin. A little self-consciously, she thought.

"Look here," George interrupted. "That answer of Phyl's wasn't quite right. Is it fair to say it's vegetable?"

"It *was* vegetable, vegetable in origin," Phyllis protested.

"Yes, but in a way it's animal too. It's *becoming* animal."

"Is it—any one's affection for any one else?" Joyce demanded promptly.

"No," said Ruth, amid general laughter.

"The difficulty with this game," said Phyllis, "is that there are so many questions you can't answer just Yes or No."

"That's why it's a good game," said George. "It's like life."

Joyce tried to recapitulate. It was in this room, associated with a person, it was vegetable in origin but becoming animal . . . but how absurd.

Perhaps they mean becoming *to* an animal, she thought.

"Is it Mrs. Granville's silver dress?"

"No."

"Is it anything to wear?"

"No."

"Is it associated with a man or a woman?"

"I can't answer that Yes or No," said George.

"Well, with a man?"

"Yes."

"Is it something I can see now?" she asked, looking directly at him.

"You're asking him twice," Martin said. "It's my turn."

Why did her mind keep straying away? Standing in the middle of the circle, she could feel them surrounding her, desiring her to divine this thing. Perhaps it was something she didn't want to guess, something that would mean——

She repeated the question, looking at Martin this time.

"No," he said, smiling.

Her mind was a blank. She went round the group again, asking almost at random. The succession of No's had a curiously numbing effect. But she knew, without having put the question directly, that it was something connected with Martin.

She came to Ben, on the last time round. She stared at his white canvas shoes, trying to think.

"Is it . . . is it——"

She turned away from the strong scent of his cigar. The glimmer of coloured light on the dining-room table caught and held her. It suggested:

"Something to do with a cake?"

"Yes," said Ben, amazed.

They were all startled, for her last attempts had been far off the track.

"Two more tries," said George, encouraging her.

She had a queer sensation that the back of her dress was open and reached unconsciously to but-

ton it. How silly, of course it's not open, it
fastens on the shoulder. . . . A cake, a
cake . . . there was a warm whiff of burning
candles in the room. She knew now what it must
be; what he had begun to tell her in the garden.
. . . They were all crowding round her, tall
people, voices coming down from above, wanting
her to explain. Two more questions . . .
one would do! Martin was standing behind
George, he looked eager and yet anxious. She remembered now: the mouse, the mouse she had
brought him; it was such a little thing; chosen and
cherished for her difficult own; and the joy of
giving away what was dearest . . . joy em-
bittered by hostile scrutiny. . . .

Everything was all tangled up together. What
had she given, a mouse to Martin or her truth to
George? Oh, the pride, the fierce pride of now
telling her pitiable secret. She could see the stripy
pattern of George's coat, she knew exactly how it
smelled. George looked eager and yet anxious——

No, George, no! her mind was crying miserably.
It wasn't you, it wasn't you; I gave it to *him*——

She must not tell them that she had guessed
it. George must be spared this last inconceivable
edge of irony; and Martin must go away before
either of them found out.

"I'm sorry," she said.   "I can't get it."
George caught her arm as she swayed.

"I don't feel very well.   Please forgive me.   I think I'll go to bed."

"I knew she wouldn't guess it," said Ruth.

"Of course it wasn't really fair," said George. "She couldn't possibly know about the slice of cake Mr. Martin had.   But it was queer how close she came."

XVI

GEORGE stood uneasily on the landing, halfway up the stair. The house seemed over-populated. Upstairs was a regular dormitory, he thought angrily: all down the long passage he could hear the stealthy movement of people going to bed: doors opening cautiously, reconnoiterings to see whether the bathroom trail was clear. And the ground floor was worse: Joyce in the sitting room filled the whole place with her presence. He could not stay in the hall, the dining room, or the porch, without being in sight or hearing of her sanctuary. Against his will he lingered on the thought of her there, the small ugly chamber transfigured by her intimacy. Even the dull brown wood of the door was different now, it thrilled him with unbearable meaning, his mind pierced through it and saw her loveliness—perhaps tormented like himself with farcical horrors. It was unbearable to think of her going away into the dark nothing of these empty hours, uncomforted. Why couldn't he go and tuck her in like one of the children? She seemed to him just that, a fright-

ened child who had somehow crept into his arms.
She was there, divided from him only by that
senseless panel. He imagined her prostrate on
the couch in a quiver of silent tears; she, exquisite,
made for delight, whose pitiful reality had shaken
his solid, well-carpentered life into this crazy totter.

My God, he reflected, I thought I had got
beyond this sort of thing.

There was a creak at the stair head; he saw her
above him, shadowy against the bay window.   In
her translucent wrap she was delicately sketched
in cloudy brightness, young and firm of outline.
So the door had been mocking him.   With a
twinge of self-disgust he shrank, stumbled down
the stairs, tiptoed out and took refuge at the far
end of the garden.

A splinter of light drew him to the table under
the pine trees.   The jug and glasses, left there
since lunch time; mutely pathetic, as forgotten
things always are.   There was still a heeltap of
tea in one of the tumblers, he drank it and found
it sirupy with sugar.   It's a mistake, he thought,
to eat sweet things late at night: they turn to sour
in the morning.   Night is the time for something
bitter.   .

In the house, yellow squares flashed on and off.
Downstairs, he could see Joyce's shadow against

the blind. At the other end of the building, in the gable, the spare-room window went dark. Martin had slipped off to bed rather oddly after their game. In the embarrassment of Joyce's momentary dizziness he had simply gone, without a word. George found himself thinking that much of the evening's difficulty was due to this bumpkin stranger. He was probably well-meaning, but either with his idiotic pleasantries or a silent smirk of censure he had a gift for blighting things. There was nothing about him that you could put precise finger on, but he had a way of making one feel guilty. How queerly, too, he had looked at Joyce.

The evening was changing. The air had shifted toward the northwest; suddenly, over the comb of the overhanging dune, a silvery spinnaker of cloud came drifting. It was like a great puff of steam, so close and silent it frightened him. For an instant, passing under the moon, this lovely island of softness darkened the night to a foggy grey. It was something strange, a secret between himself and the weather, encouraging his silly wits not to be afraid of the desperate magic of fancy, the fear and tenderness hidden in men's hearts.

He turned again toward the house, and saw that now Joyce's window was black. She was there,

at rest; he blessed her being in that little room.
He had thought of it only as opening into the main
thoroughfare of the house; but it was open, too,
into the garden and freedom   What did the door
matter! She was there, shining. He could speak
to her. He imagined her voice, her trembling
husky whisper, when she heard him at the sill.
Why is kindness always whispered, while anger is
so loud? How delightful if people shouted "I love
you!" as though it were an insult. Glorious, to
stand under the window and halloo it at her, watch
the house rouse with scandalized life! Ah, what
friends we might have been if they hadn't made us
whisper. Why did they force us to be lovers?

Then he remembered—the accurate circumstantial memory of the householder. The window
was screened. To speak to her through a wire
mesh—intolerable. Besides, it might only make
matters worse. He could never tell her his own
joy, and might merely smirch hers. They might
only struggle dumbly in the grotesque antic of
spirits whose moods cannot mingle. The moment
had passed. Life had gone by him, while he was
fretting over paltry trifles, and left him a drudge.
There was nothing to do but go indoors and work
on the booklet. How exciting that brochure would
be, what marvellous advertising, if he could

really tell what summer was like at the Island. Why, the company would have to run special trains. The very aisles would be packed, people sitting on up-ended suitcases, if they knew that this dangerous coast was the place where Temptation really broke through . . . where the old Demiurge laid his cards on the table. It would become a Resort—yes, an asylum for lunatics, people ridiculed by transfusions of the moon. How a poet might write it, telling the colour of that world. Warm tawny flanks of sand hills, sprawled like panthers. The sun a coal of topaz, veiled in white flame that sheeted the whole summit of sky. Light so fierce one never looked upward. Wherever one turned was a burning and a glitter; the air was a lens and gathered all its rays into one stream. Always one's knuckles were sweet with salty smell. Repressed thunder yawning in the blue elixir of the afternoon: deep, deep afternoon, penetrated with lawless beauty. The small sorry whisper of the wind sang it in the keen scimitar grasses; smooth beams of driftwood, faded by the sea, felt it; the sandpipers, drunk with it, staggered on twiggy legs. Bronzed thighs and shoulders, shining in the green shallows marbled with foam. . . .

The transitive billow of cloud slipped away

beyond the roof; again the strong resinous air was
clarified, streamed with gracious light. His mind
almost smiled at his fatuity: the sentiment did not
graduate into an actual smile, but spent itself in a
tiny whiff of self-deprecation through his nostrils.
He stretched upward, raising his arms, standing
tiptoed, feeling the calf-tendons tighten and coolness in his fingers as the blood sank. His hands
met a low limb that reached across his head. He
gripped it and chinned himself. There was good
animal satisfaction in feeling the quiver in the
biceps, the hanging weight of his body. Well,
we're not done for yet, he said to himself. No, sir,
not yet. He capered a few dance steps on the silky
floor of needles, and pulled out his pipe. . . .

She was coming. He saw her coming, swiftly
across the lawn. No, not swiftly; evenly was the
word; unquestioningly; as he had always known
she would come. His mouth was open to warn her
of the croquet hoops, but she passed surely among
them. When he saw her face, he knew this was
something not to be spoiled by words. Her face
was enough.

In that unreasonable glamour she was pure fable:
the marble (Oh, too cold, too hard a word) come
to life. There was no pang, no trouble, no desire;

he knew only that there is some answer to the gorgeous secret: the secret that the world is in conspiracy to deny—— No, not to deny; more cunning than that: to admit and pass heedless on. There was meaning in everything; significance in the shapes of things. The black plumes and pinnacles of the trees were fashioned exactly so, could never have been otherwise.

They were away from rooms and roofs. They were on the beach; the tide was far ebbed, they ran over mirrors of sand, they were in sparkling black water milder than air. Still there were no words; their white bodies gleamed in silver, laved in snowy fans of surf. They were just themselves, chafing impediments were gone; nothing was between them and they wanted nothing. They ran, breathing warmly, to burrow in the powdery cliff, where the acid smell of sharp grasses sifted down from the dunes. They lay in a hollow of sand; she curled against him, nestled smoothly close, he could feel her thrilling with small quivers of joy. There was no pang, no trouble, no desire; only peace.

Everything else they had ever known had been only an interruption. This had always been happening, underneath. It was the unknown music for which their poem had been written. They were quit of the pinch of Time, the facetious

II

nudge of Custom. Quietness was in them, satient
like fresh water in a thirsty throat. Here was
the fulfilment men plot and swink for: and how
different from crude anticipation. What could
there be now but pity and kindness? Here was
triumph: Man, the experimenting artist, had
created fantasy above the grasp of his audience,
Nature. Like any true artist, he must always
play a little above his audience's head.

"Now I'm going to tell you the truth," he said
happily, and waited a moment for the luxury of
her voice.

She was silent. He turned to look; her face was
anxious.

"Why is it," he said gently, "that when you announce you're going to tell the truth, people always
expect something disagreeable?"

Then he knew that the sand was chill and gritty.
A breeze was blowing, the light was dim and
meagre. This was not the glad forgiving sun but
the cold and glassy moon.

"No, no!" she cried. "You must never tell
the truth in a dream. If you do . . . it
happens."

"But this was a lovely truth," he began. A
window snapped into brightness beside him, just

above his head. Phyllis was looking from the pantry.

"George! What on earth are you muttering about out there? Come in and help me cut sandwiches."

XVII

HE WAS startled to find Phyllis at work in her nightgown. Another hallucination, perhaps, he thought sardonically. Everything seems to burlesque everything else.

. She had thrown aside her blue quilted wrapper and was busy slicing and spreading. The table was crowded with bread, ham, beef, lettuce, mustard, jam, and cheese. The Picnic. George had forgotten the menace of the Picnic. It struck him as pathetic to see her valiantly preparing the details of this festival which was already doomed and damned. She was chopping off little brown corners of crust. Wasteful, as usual; besides, the crust is the best part. He managed not to say so, remembering that he had made the remark every time he had ever seen her cut sandwiches. The lace yoke at her neck had two tiny buds of blue ribbon stitched in it. There was something pitiably nuptial about them   How soft and young she was in her flimsy robe. Her eyes were smudged with fatigue. How beautiful she would have looked to any other man.

"My dear child, cutting sandwiches in your best nightgown."

"I haven't anything better to do in it, have I?"

"Yes, you have. Go to bed in it."

He held the wrapper for her.

"Put this on. I'll open the door. Whew, it's hot in here. I'll finish all this for you."

The blade of the long carving knife continued, small definite crunches.

"You can have your sardines. I found a box in the pantry. There isn't any key for them, you'll have to use the can opener.",

The warm kitchen air was like a stupor. This was the steady heart of the house. Ghostly moonlight might wash up to the sill, fragile fancies pervade other rooms: here strong central life went calmly on. In the range red coals slept deep, covered and nourished for the long night. The tall boiler, its silvery paint flaked and dulled, gave off drowsy heat. Under the table the cat Virginia, who was not to be shocked, lay solidly upright with her paws tucked in, sated with scraps and vibrating a strong stupid purr. The high grimed ceiling was speckled with motionless flies, roosting there after a hard day. Packages of groceries, series of yellow bowls and platters, were ranged on the shelves in comfortable order. This was not a

modern kitchen, shiny, white and sterile, like a
hospital. It was old, ugly, inconvenient, strong
with the memory of meals arduously prepared;
meals of long ago, for people now vanished.

"The weather's changing," he said. "I don't
know if to-morrow will be fine or not."

He wondered at himself: able to speak so lightly,
as if everything was usual. His mind was still
trudging back, up clogging sand hills, from a
phantom bend of shore.

"If it rains, we'll have our sandwiches at home.
I've promised Lizzie the day off."

He saw a quick horrible picture of the Picnic
spread in the dining room, rain driving outside, the
children peevish, themselves angrily mute.

"There's cold chicken in the ice box; please get
it out and slice it for salad sandwiches. I don't
think Mr. Martin cares much for beef, I noticed
at lunch."

"What does he think he is? Some kind of
Messiah? If he doesn't like our ways, what did he
come butting in for?"

He checked himself. The moment was ripe for
quarrel, the gross mustard-sharpened air seemed
to suggest it. He put the carcass of fowl on the
scrubbed drain board by the sink and began to

carve. Standing so, his back was toward her.
He made some pretext to turn, hoping to divine
her mood; but her face was averted. There was
ominous restraint in the shape of her back. The
anticlimax of all this, the delicatessen-shop smell,
after his ecstasy in the garden, fretted his nerves.
Brutal shouts of wrath clamoured in his mind. It
was infuriating to see her so appealing: can't one
ever get away from it, must a man love even his
wife? He wanted to ask her this, but feared she
would miss the humour of it. He longed to horrify
her with his rage, so that he could get rid of it and
then show the tenderness he secretly felt. Certainly I'm the colossus of sentimentalists, he
thought. I can turn directly from one kind of love
to another. Queer, the way it looks now it's my
feeling for Joyce that is disinterested and pure, my
love for Phyl that's really carnal. How did this
morality business get so mixed up?

He amused himself by putting the slivers of
chicken in two piles: the dark meat for Martin, the
white for Joyce. How white she had been in the
surf. . . . But that was only a dream. This
is real, this is earnest. This is Now, I'm cutting
sandwiches for the Picnic. This is what Time is
doing to me; what is it doing to her? How did our

two Times get all knotted up together? He found himself affectionately stroking a smooth slice of chicken breast.

There was something in Phyllis's silence that pricked him. He looked uneasily over his shoulder. She had sat down in the chair by the table, her chin leaning on one wrist, watching him. He went to her and touched her shoulder gently.

"Go to bed, Phyl dear."

"George, can't we get away from this house?"

"What on earth do you mean?"

"Get away. Take me away, George; we'll take the children and go. To-night. Before anybody wakes up."

She rose suddenly.

"I'm frightened. Take me away. George, I can't live through to-morrow, not if it's like to-day."

Just the way I feel, he thought.

"There, there, little frog, you're all frazzled out. It'll be all right, don't worry. Go and get your sleep."

"No, I'm not tired. I wish I were. I'm all burning up with *not* being tired. George, we could take the babies and just get in the car and go. Go anywhere, anywhere where there isn't anybody.—We'll take Miss Clyde with us if you like. She's frightened too."

"Don't be absurd."

"George, it would be such fun; when they all came down to breakfast, Ben and Ruth and Mr. Martin, we just wouldn't be here. Never come back, never see this place again."

"You're raving, Phyl. Why, I took this house specially for you. Besides, you know I can't go away now, I've got this booklet to finish."

She looked so miserable, so desperate, his anger began to throb.

"You can write a booklet about something else. You know you can, they're all crazy to get your stuff. George, you're so big and clever, you can do anything. Miss Clyde can illustrate it. I don't mind your loving her, I'll be sensible, just take us away before the Picnic. Go and wake her now, she can go in her wrapper, you'll like that."

"Damnation," he burst out, "don't talk such tripe. I believe you're crazy. It's this half-wit Martin who's got on your nerves. I've got a mind to wake *him* up, throw him out of the house. What the devil did you ask him in for?"

"It's my fault. But he's changed so, since this morning. We've all changed. We're not the same people we were."

H*

She pushed her arms up inside the sleeves of his coat and caught his elbows. He remembered that cherished way of hers, unconscious appeal to old tendernesses. He looked down on the top of her head, into the warm hollow where his head had lain. Her neck's prettier than Joyce's, he thought bitterly.

"It's queer *you* should hate him so," she said.

"What do you mean?" He pulled his arms away.

"Oh, I don't know what I mean. Perhaps he— perhaps he *is* what you said."

"What, a half-wit?"

"A kind of Messiah. They come to make silly people unhappy, don't they?"

He looked at her in cold amazement and disgust. Only a few moments ago he had been afraid of her; but now, by showing her poor thoughts, she had put herself at his mercy.

"You go to bed," he said. "I'm sick of this nonsense." He gripped her shoulders roughly and pushed her toward the door.

"Please, just let me put away the sandwiches. I want to wrap them in wet napkins so they'll keep fresh."

"Forget the damn sandwiches."

"Not damn, *ham* sandwiches." She couldn't

help laughing. It was so paltry to have him pro-
pelling her like a punishable child.

"Ham, jam, or damn, forget them!" he cried,
raging. "You and your Messiah have ruined
this Picnic anyhow. You spoiled it because you
knew I looked forward to it. You've plotted
against it, sneered at me and at Joyce because you
knew I admired her."

"Admired her! Oh, is that the word?"

The little sarcasm hummed like a tuning fork
in some silent chamber of his mind.

"You fool," he said. "Are you trying to push
her into my arms?"

"I guess she can find the way without pushing."

"Well, you *are* a fool," he said slowly, in a dull
voice that struck her deeper than any temper
could have done. "You throw away love as if it
was breadcrusts."

With a furious sweep he was about to hurl the
neat piles of her handiwork on the floor. In one
last salvage of decency he altered the course of his
hand. He seized a fistful of the little brown strips
of crust and flung them wildly across the room.
The carving knife clattered off the table.

"You're frightening Virginia," was all she said.

Anger, the red and yellow clown, burst through
the tight paper hoop of his mind and played gro-

tesque unlaughable capers. Bewildered by his own ferocity he strode to the corner, swung open the door of the back stairs, and pointed savagely upward. She went without another word. Her blue eyes were very large and dark, they faced him with the unwavering defiance he detested and admired. Good old Phyl, he couldn't help thinking. She's unbeatable. Now, as usual, he had put himself in the wrong. He crashed the door behind her, and stood listening to her slow steps.

He soothed the cat with some sardine-tails, finished making the chicken sandwiches, wrapped them carefully as Phyllis had suggested. I wonder what we'll be thinking when we eat them? As he put them away in the ice box he noticed the cocoanut cake on a shelf. With a sense of retaliation he cut himself a thick slice. He became aware of the scrambling tick of the alarm clock on the dresser. A quarter past eleven. The house was thrillingly still. The serenely dormant kitchen slowly sobered the buffoon dancing in his brain.

He fetched his precious bottle of Sherwood and poured a minim dose. The golden drug saluted him gently. In this fluid too the flagrant miracle lay hidden, the privy atom of truth and fury. The guest of honour, he thought ironically, feeling his vitals play host to that courteous warmth.

The guest of honour, always expelled. A spark
falls into your soul. Shall you cherish it, shelter
it to clear consuming flame; or shall you hurry to
stamp it out? Can a man take fire in his bosom
and his clothes not be burned? The smell of
burning cloth is mighty disagreeable. Vacantly
he studied the label on the bottle. *Manufactured
prior to Jan. 17, 1920. These spirits were tax paid
at the non-beverage rate* FOR MEDICINAL PURPOSES
ONLY. *Sale or use for other purposes will subject
the seller or user to very heavy penalties.* Well,
certainly this is a Medicinal Use, he thought.
"If ever a seaman wanted drugs, it's me." Where
did the phrase come from? . . . Yes, old
Billy Bones, in *Treasure Island.*

Well, these foolishnesses would have blown over
by to-morrow. Do a little work on the booklet
and then turn in. He must get the thing done,
earn some money. The gruesome burden of
expenses. How little Phyllis realizes the load a
man's mind carries. I suppose she carries one
too, poor child. Every mind carries the weight
of the whole world.

He was on hands and knees, picking up the
scraps of crust that had fallen under the boiler.
In a luxurious self-pity he found himself humming
a hymn tune. Blessed solitude, where a man can

sing to himself and admire the sweet sorrow of
his own cadence! An almost forgotten poem came
into his head and fitted pleasantly to the air.

The Silver Girl she came to me when spring was
    dancing green,
She said, "I've come to wait on you and keep your
    cabin clean;
To wash your face and hands and feet, and make your
    forehead cool—
I'll get you into Heaven yet, you Damned Old Fool!

Something in this appealed nicely to his mood.
He allowed himself an encore. His voice, rising
behind the stove, got a good resonance. Then he
heard a footfall, a door opening. Ah, he thought,
Phyl has come down to say she's sorry for being
so crude. Well, I'll let her speak first. I'm tired
of always being the one to make advances.

He waited, industriously gathering crusts,
though he felt that the posture of Lazarus was not
advantageous. There was no word.

"Well," he said impatiently, "have you had
enough of your funny business?"

He turned, and saw Nounou's amazed face in
the aperture of the back door. With an incoherent
murmur he rose, took his bottle, and stalked out of
the kitchen.

XVIII

IT WOULD be interesting to speculate," said page 38 of George's treatise, "how such a cheery little town obtained the name Dark Harbour. Perhaps it was due to the scenic background of rugged hills that overlooks the picturesque old fishing port and reflects its invigorating pine woods in the water. At any rate, the future of the place is bright indeed. The Eastern Railroad's express service now stops there, and large metropolitan interests have pledged themselves to the erection of a modern caravansary which will supplement the long famous 'folksy' hospitality of the Bayview Hotel. Separated only by a lengthy trestle from the mainland, the Island spreads its varied allure of rolling sand dunes, pine groves, and broad shallow beaches. Shaped like a crescent, its outward curve is buffeted by the mighty ocean; on the inner side, sheltered from easterly gales by the unique sand hills, is the comfortable cottage colony where a number of wise people have been vacationing for many years. Many artists have discovered the pictorial charm

of the region, and find in the forests or in the mari-
time life of the Bay subjects for their water colours
and oils.   Canvases that have later become famous
in academies and exhibitions have first felt the
brush in those shingled studios clustered about the
old inn, renowned for its savoury chowder.   There
is a brilliance in the air, an almost Italian richness
of colour, in the Island's landscape.   It will be
many years before so vast a terrain can become
crowded, but many new bungalows have been
built lately, and the newcomers pay tribute to the
good taste of those who, a generation agone, divined Dark Harbour's magic as a haven of summer
tranquillity."

He felt a rational pride in this composition.   It
was in the genially fulsome vein esteemed by railroad companies.   Even if people weren't tranquil,
in a place so competently described, they ought to
be.   He thought there was a neatness in that
touch about Dark Harbour and its bright future.
Phyllis was probably right when she often said it
was a shame Mr. Granville should spend his talents
in mere publicity work when he might so easily
write something famous—fiction, for instance.
These are my fictions, he always replied, pointing
to his private shelf of advertising pamphlets, neatly bound and gilded as his Works.

He had spread out his papers on the dining table, where he could write without seeing Joyce's door. But he couldn't seem to resume the flow of that slick treacly style, which the experienced brochurist can smoothly decant, like a tilted molasses barrel. The discomforting irony of the last word penetrated him. He changed "Italian richness" to "Italian passion," but that was as far as inspiration carried him. It was vain to remind himself that Walter Scott had written novels all night long, that Napoleon had planned campaigns in the agony of stomach-ache, that Elbert Hubbard was never at a loss for a Little Journey. In a nervous fidget he pared his nails, sharpened pencils, rearranged the glasses on the sideboard, emptied Ben's cigar débris from the living-room ash tray. He trod stealthily, in stocking feet, for fear of disturbing Joyce. Without his usual couch to sleep on, his usual table to work at, he felt homeless. There was a dull pain at the bottom of his ribs. He tried to remember whether he had unduly bolted his food at dinner. Perhaps he was going to have appendicitis.

He had a sort of insane desire to justify his existence, to atone for a day of such incredible futility by getting some work done. If every possible extraneous trifle could be attended to perhaps his mind might be calmed. He crept upstairs to clean his teeth and found that Phyllis had put his dressing gown and pyjamas and slippers on the window seat. Was that a softening overture, or a hint that she did not want him in the bedroom? He tiptoed warily to the balcony to glance at the children. Even in sleep Sylvia was still the coquette: she lay with one hand curled against her cheek, the most ravishing pose, her face a lovely fragile gravity. Janet was restless, muttering something about bathing.

He undressed, sitting on the window seat. With a vague notion of postponing the struggle with the pamphlet he went through his routine with unusual care, watching the details. He noticed for the first time his ingenious attempt to retain the tip of each sock, by curling his toes into it as he removed it. The purpose was evidently to turn the sock completely inside out in the one motion of stripping it off. For the first time in weeks he decided to fold his trousers neatly instead of just throwing them on a chair. He gave them a preliminary shake and found that the sand lodged in the cuffs flew unerringly into his eyes. He discovered that if he tried to put the left leg into his pyjamas first, instead of the right, it didn't feel as though he had them on at all. The laundress had managed to let the end of the waist-string vanish inside its little tunnel of hem. It required some very sharp work to creep it out again. What a good booklet could be written, for some pyjama and underwear manufacturer, on The Technique of Getting Undressed. How pleasant that if you lay out your clothes just in the order of their discarding they are exactly serialized in the correct sequence for dressing to-morrow.

All this, he felt with subtle horror, was just a postponement of something inevitable, something he knew was coming but could not identify. Some great beauty of retribution had him in its onward march. He was unworthy of the glory of living, he had niggled and haggled and somewhere in his bunglings he had touched some fatal spring. He had broken some seal, let the genie out of the bottle. The little whiff of fragrant vapour had flowed and spread until it darkened the whole sky. It hung terrible above him and the four tiny Georges cowered beneath it. And behind and within every other thought was Joyce. He could see her, perfect, inaccessible, afraid. This dear device of Nature, this gay, simple ingenuity of dividing life into halves and making them hanker for one another! Oh, Joyce, Joyce, it *does* matter. Joyce, I need you so.

A craven impulse tempted him to turn in at once, on the window seat; but its curved shape was not comfortable; moreover, how could he possibly sleep? Downstairs the big couch had a lamp by it; he could read, and while reading, think. The principal pleasure of reading, he had always found, is to fix the attention of the coarse outer mind, allowing the inner faculty to slip free. As he went down the clock startled him by counting midnight. He timed his step on the creaky treads so that the chime would cover them. But that settled it, he thought. One can *continue* working after twelve, but one can't possibly begin work at that hour. Besides, it's impossible to be conscientious in dressing gown and slippers. Morals, conscience, ambition, all the cunning artifice of custom, are laid aside with the garments of the day. The sophistries of virtue avail you nothing now. The thing in your heart that you are angriest at and most ashamed of, that is God. And that's what gods are invented for: to be despised and rejected. A god who was honoured and welcomed, how unhappy he would be.

He lay down on the couch with a book, but his mind ran wild behind the printed lines. The weight and breathing of the silent house pressed about him. How well he knew that feeling of a house at night. All the others, broken at last by the day's long war of attrition, lost in their silence; himself the sole survivor, gleaning stupidly over the battlefield. Matching his lonely wit against destiny, aware of a shuddering compassion for these unruly lives under his charge. What was it that kept them all going? Only his dreams, his poor busy ideas. For the moment he could feel the whole fabric transfigured with truth and tenderness; with love that was furious and clean, with work that was sane and absorbing. What did he really care whether thousands of people did or did not spend their summer on the Great Scenic Route of the Eastern Railroad? Or whether they bedded on the Morrison Mattress, that Makes Sleep a Career?

He slipped to his knees beside the sofa, but he could not even pray. He was aware of the door behind him, and of Phyllis in the room overhead. How terrible if any one should find him on his knees. Praying is only respectable if done in congregations. He remembered those cold evenings long ago, when he and Phyllis couldn't sleep unless she were pressed close behind him, her arm across his chest. And now he was living among strangers. I'll do whatever you tell me, I'll do whatever you tell me. But by heaven he had glimpsed it: he had seen beauty within breath and grasp: too close to mar it by selfishness.   No, said his demon, you shan't even have the consolation of fine words. You shall have all the mockery and none of the bliss.

I suppose biology's pulling my leg, he reflected. . . .

He must have been kneeling there a long time. His forehead was numb from pressing on the ridged tapestry of the couch.   At least you don't need the light on when you're trying to pray.   The bills are big enough as it is.   He rose stiffly and snicked off the current.

At the foot of the stair he paused.   If Joyce were awake he might hear her stir.   His hand gripped the carved newel, then slid onto the smooth ascent of the banister rail.   He stood a moment, and turned away.

The bedroom was dim.   The blinds were not all the way down, dregs of that sparkling moonlight flowed underneath.   Phyllis was asleep, he could see her head against the white linen.   She lay as she always did, at the far side of the bed, turned away from the door, her arms crossed, one hand perching on her shoulder, the other tucked under the pillow. He went softly round the foot of the bed, stepping aside to avoid her slippers. He knew by instinct exactly where they would be.

Crouched at the bedside, he slid one arm under the pillow to find her hand. His fingers met a small damp handkerchief.

He gathered her into his arms. Out of some far-off vacancy she moved drowsily and welcomed him home. They knew every curve of their old embrace. Here was no fear and no doubting. Here was his consolation. Who was ever more beautiful? The tiny flattened handkerchief, was it not a pathetic symbol of the bruised mercies of love? Ah, be slow to mock the plain, simplest things: good-byes, angers, fidelities, renunciations.

He held her close and more close. Then, with a gruesome pang, he checked the name that was on his lips. In the poor comedy of his heart there was room for but one thought: gratitude to Joyce; Joyce who in the unstained bravery of her spirit had taught him anew the worth and miracle of love and whose only reward had been suffering. Her name, so long echoed in his unuttered voice, now filled his mind and terrified him. Here, with Phyllis in his arms, he was thinking of her; this frail ghost of passion came between them. In

physical sickness his embrace grew faint.   It could
not be: the last scruple of his manhood revolted
against this consummate deceit.

Still half in dream, Phyllis divined him laggard.
She crept closer.   "Oh, Martin, Martin," she
whispered.   "I knew you'd come."

Now he knew where the dark current of the
hours had been bearing him.   Nothing else was
possible.   Quietly, without anger or surprise, in
the relief of one free to face his destiny, he left
the room and went down the stair.   His hand was
out to turn the knob when he saw that Joyce's
door was opening toward him.

XIX

JOYCE lay in a trance of weariness. A nervous tremolo shivered up and down from her knees to her stomach; her spirit seemed lost and dragged under into the strange circling life of the body, stubborn as that of a tree, that goes on regardless of the mind. I don't care, she thought, I'm glad I'm alive. She was too inert to close her hot eyes or turn over into the pillow to shut out sounds from her sharpened ears. She heard George's step on the garden path, Phyllis come downstairs and go to the kitchen. Beneath everything else was the obbligato of the house itself; twinges of loose timbers, the gurgle and rush of plumbing, creak of beds, murmuring voices, soft shut of doors. Tenacious life reluctantly yielding itself to oblivion. Then into this fading recessional came the low sough in the pines, the slackening volleys of the crickets like a besieging army that had withdrawn its troops. And the far-away cry of a train. She imagined it, trailing panes of golden light along the shore, or perhaps darkly curtained sleeping cars partitioned into narrow kennels where mysterious people lay alone: and the bursting silver plume of its whistle, spirting into the cool night, tearing a jagged rent in silence, shaking the whole membrane of elastic air that enveloped them all, a vibration that came undulating over the glittering bay, over the lonely beaches, trembled beside her and went throbbing away. . . . She hadn't been down to the beach yet, past the rolling dunes that gave her childhood a first sense of fatal solitude. She tried to remember how that shore looked: wideness, sharp air, the exact curved triangle of sails leaning into unseen sweetness of breeze, steep slides of sand over-tufted above by toppling clumps of grass. If one could escape down there and go bathing in moonlight; come back cleansed, triumphant.

The whisper at the window sill startled her. She knew Bunny at once.

"You must get him away. Before it's too late, before he knows."

Joyce understood perfectly; so perfectly it didn't seem necessary to say anything. This was just what she had been telling herself.

She nodded.

"I kept calling him while you were all in the

living room. I was here at this window. He won't listen. He thinks I'm just teasing him."

Joyce remembered Martin closing the door.

"Then I called *you*. I was so afraid you wouldn't hear me. It's awful to be helpless."

"Bunny, you're not helpless. Tell me what to do."

"What room is he in?"

"I don't know. Yes, I do, I think it's at the end of the passage, next the bath."

"The old nursery. Oh, if I could come indoors. I can't; they've forgotten me."

"We'll manage," Joyce whispered. "I always knew you and I would have to help each other."

"He must find something to take him back. You are the one who can help."

Joyce knew there was some secret here too beautiful to be said. Bunny could not tell her, it must be guessed.

"Is it something I gave him?"

"Something you'd like to keep."

"Is it the mouse? Bunny, how can we find it? That was a lifetime ago."

"Perhaps it's in the nursery. In the old toy cupboard."

"I'll get it in the morning."

"That may be too late. Now, to-night."

"Oh Bunny, tell me plainly. Is it the mouse you mean?"

She was tugging fiercely to raise the screen, jammed in its grooves. Her fingers still tingled from the sharp edges of the shallow metal sockets. Only the empty garden, the sinking candy-peel moon beyond the black arc of hill.

The impression was vivid upon her. There was only one thing to do, she must go through the sleeping house to Martin's room, rouse him, tell him at once. She rose from bed and opened the door.

He was there, holding out his hand; motionless as though he had been waiting so all the shining night. She took it mechanically.

"Who is it?" she said.

"Who else could it be?"

But at first she had thought it was Martin, somehow warned by Bunny. They stood aghast of one another, in silence, awkwardly holding hands. It was not like a meeting, it was like a good-bye.

The declining moonlight limned her cloudily. But this was no silly dream. He saw her revealed in all her wistful beauty, meant from the beginning for him.

"George, we must get Martin out of the house——"

Martin again.   Evidently, he thought, the gods intend to wring the last drop of comedy out of me.

"Damn Martin," he said softly.   "Joyce, I didn't find you at last to talk about *him*.   Dear, I told you we'd know it if the time came."

Was this what Bunny meant by giving?   I have nothing to give.   The Me he loves has gone somewhere.   How can I tell him?   Instead of the imagined joy and communion there's only horror.   And I want so to love him.

He had carried her to the couch and was kneeling beside her.   Oh, if I could lay down the burden of this heavy, heavy love.   If I could love him gladly, not just bitterly.   Is this the only way to save him from knowing?   Such a little thing, that I wanted to keep for myself.   She turned from him convulsively and buried her face in the pillow. He mustn't see my tears.   The cruellest thing is he'll think I don't love him.   No man was ever so loved.   But I gave myself, long ago, to the dream of him.   I can't mix it with the reality.

She turned, in a mercy of pure tenderness.

"George, dear George, I meant what I said."

I'll do whatever you tell me, I'll do whatever you tell me.   But he divined her misery.   The brave words trembled.   She lay before him, white, inaccessible, afraid.   Exquisite, made for delight.

with every grace that the brave lust of man has
dreamed; and weariness, anxiety, some strange
disease of the spirit, frustrated it. Their love too
was a guest of honour, a god to be turned away.
She lay there, her sweet body the very sign and
symbol of their need, and he knew nothing but
pity, as for a wounded child. In that strange
moment his poor courage was worthy of hers.
God pity me for a fool, he thought. But I love
her best of all because I shall never have her.

"I'm going to tell you the truth," he began——

A jarring crash shook the house, followed by a
child's scream. He rose heavily to his feet, tightened and nauseated with terror. He knew exactly
what must have happened. The railing on the
sleeping porch, which he had forgotten to mend.
One of the children had got out of bed, stumbled
against it, the rotten posts had given way. If she
had fallen from that height . . . he pictured
a broken white figure on the gravel. This was his
punishment for selfishness and folly. Oh, it is
always the innocent who suffer.

With heaviness in his feet he hurried through the
dining room and veranda. All was still: looking
up he could see the balcony unaltered. Then,
through the open windows above he heard the

unmistakable clang of metal on a wooden floor. Ben's bed.

Unable to shake off his conviction of disaster he ran upstairs. Phyllis was crouching in the passage, comforting Janet. "I had a bad dream," the child sobbed, "then there was that awful noise."

"There, there, darling, you're all right now. We all have dreams sometimes. You can come into bed with Mother."

There was the bleat of one of the talking dolls. "*Maaa-Maa!*" it cried, and Sylvia appeared, sleepily stolid. "Is it to-morrow?" she asked.

"I thought the porch had broken down," said Phyllis hysterically. "George, did you fix that railing?"

"Nonsense. The porch is all right. Get back to sleep, little toads."

"What was it, Ben's bed?"

"Ben's! No such luck, it's mine," said Ruth, opening the door. "Where does the light turn on? I can't find the button." She saw George and gave a squeak of dismay.

She needn't be so damned skittish, he thought angrily. Nightgowns don't seem to be any novelty in this house. "Phyl, you take Janet into bed, I'll put Sylvia on the window seat. Keep them off that porch till I've mended the railing in the morning."

Ben was grumbling over the wreckage. "George, what's the secret of this thing? Lend a hand."

"I'm frightfully sorry," said George. "I ought to have warned you. Here, I can fix it, there's a bit of clothes line——"

"For Heaven's sake, don't start tinkering now," said Ruth, who had dived into the other bed. "I'm all right here, and Ben can sleep on the mattress."

Her door was open, she stood anxiously waiting as he came downstairs at last. She had put on her wrapper, he noticed with a twinge.

"Ruth's bed had a blow-out," he said. "At least I thought *she* was safe when she's between the sheets." He felt that he ought to want to laugh, but he had no desire to. I suppose it's because I've got no sense of humour. "Mr. Martin seems the only one who knows that night is meant to forget things in. Well, let him sleep. He'll be on his way early in the morning."

She did not answer at once, searching for the words that would help him most.

"I must go too. George, you must let me. I'd only spoil your Picnic."

"You'll miss a lot of nice sandwiches," he said bitterly. "I made them myself, white meat."

With divine perception she saw the nature of his wound, the misery of his shame and self-abasement. It was not love of her he needed now, but love of himself, to keep life in him.

"We wouldn't have any chance to be *us*, we couldn't talk, we must say it now."

He remembered that once they had promised themselves they would never say it.

"It's better so, I suppose. Then there won't be even one sorrow that we haven't shared."

"Sorrow?" she said. "Let's call it joy. Dear, I shall always worship you as the bravest and most generous I have ever known. To do without things one can't have, what credit is that? But to do without what one might have had . . . George, let me try to get a little rest. I feel so ill."

He tucked her in and patted her shoulder.

"Good-night, dear," he said. "Don't worry. Everything will be all right in the morning. God bless you. . . . Don't forget any of the things I haven't told you."

She knew that this was as near being one of his Moments as he could be expected to manage. He had turned the corner, at least three of the Georges

I

would live. And the Fourth—well, she had that
one where nothing mortal now could blot or stain
him. For ever.

"In the morning" . . . it was morning
already. As he lay down on the couch he could
feel, rather than see, the first dim fumes of day.
The brief hush and interim was over, the pink
moon had gone. The last of the crickets flung the
password to the birds, treetops began to warble.
A new link in the endless chain picked up the tension of life. Somewhere over the hillside a cock
was crowing his brisk undoubting cheer.

So this was what they called victory. What was
the saying?—— One more such victory. . . .
Not even those last merciful words of hers could
acquit him of his own damnation. All the irony,
none of the bliss. The world hung about his neck
like the Mariner's dead albatross. The charnel
corpse clung to him, rotting, with bony skull and
jellied festering eye. But even the Mariner was
worthier, having killed the bird; he himself had
only maimed it. There would not even be the
sharp numbing surgery of good-bye. Endlessly,
through long perspectives of pain, he could see
themselves meeting, smiling and parting, to en-
counter once more round the next corner of mem-

ory and all the horror to be lived again. We're
experienced in partings, he had said once.

The gradual summer dawn crept up the slopes
of earth, brimmed and brightened, and tinctures
of lavender stained the sweetened air. The hours
when sleep is happiest, ere two and two have
waked to find themselves four, and the birds pour
the congested music of night out of their hearts.
And the day drew near: the day when men are so
reasonable, canny, and well-bred; when colour
comes back to earth and beneficent weary necessities resume; the healthful humorous day, the
fantastic day that men do well to take so seriously
as it distracts them from their unappeasable desires. With an unheard buzz of cylinders the
farmer's flivver twirled up the back lane and
brought the morning milk.

XX

JANET was surprised to find that she had gone abroad during the night. She was puzzled until she noticed that where she lay she could see herself reflected in the dressing-table mirror, which was tilted forward a little. The shoehorn, that held it at the proper angle for Mother's hair, had slipped down. So the whole area of the big bed was visible in the glass, and the mounded hill of white blanket that must be Mother. Under the snug tent of bedclothes Janet could feel the radiating warmth coming from behind her. She experimented a little, edging softly closer to see how near she could get to that large heat without actually touching it. How warm grown-up people's bodies are!

The curtains rippled inward in the cool morning air. The light was very grey, not yellow as it ought to be on the morning of a picnic. Her clothes were on the floor beside the bed. Clothes look lonely with nobody in them. She watched herself in the glass, opening her mouth and holding up her hand to see the reflection do the same thing.

Then the clock downstairs struck seven, and she felt it safe to slip out. In the glass she saw the blankets open, a pair of legs grope outward. Cautiously, not to rouse Mother, she picked up her clothes and got to the door. As she turned the knob one shoe fell with a thump. She looked anxiously at the rounded hill. It stirred ominously, but said nothing.

Sylvia, with sheets and blankets trailing from her, lay like a bundle of laundry on the window seat. Janet woke her, they sat dressing and babbling together, now and then shouting along the passage to Rose, who slept with Nounou. Rose kept opening the nursery door to ask what they said, then, while the remark was being repeated, Nounou's voice would command her to shut it. Janet, with brown knees hunched under her chin, picked at shoelace knots. Sylvia, in her deliberate way, was planning this time to get her shirt on right side forward. She announced several times her intention of drinking plenty of ginger ale at the Picnic, because peanut butter sandwiches make you so thirsty. She kept saying this in the hope of learning, from Janet's comment, whether milk has to be drunk at Picnics. Janet did not contradict her, so Sylvia felt that the ginger ale was a probability.

Ruth, lying in a delicious morning drowse, rather enjoyed their clatter, as one does enjoy the responsibilities of others. Refreshed by long slumber, she relished the seven-o'clock-in-the-morning feeling of a house with children in it. A sharp rumour of bacon and coffee came tingling up the back stairs. She lazily reckoned the number of people who would be using the bathroom. It would be a good plan to get ahead of the traffic. But while she was trying to make the decision she heard the children hailing George. He said something about not leaning out of the windows without any clothes on. "We're trying to see if there are cobwebs on the lawn, when there's cobwebs it's not going to rain." Then his steps moved along the corridor. She relapsed into her warm soothing sprawl. Besides, it's always a nuisance to get down too early and have to wait about for breakfast. She liked to arrive just when the coffee was coming fresh onto the table.

She looked forward to an entertaining day. Nothing is more amusing than one's friends in the knot of absurd circumstance. She had been afraid of Joyce; but certainly last night the girl had made a fool of herself. And Phyllis, the cool and lovely Phyllis, usually so sure, she too would be on the defensive. The life of women like Ruth

sometimes appears a vast campaign of stealth.
They move like Guy Fawkes conspirators in the
undervaults of society, planting ineffective petards
in one another's cellars.

She enjoyed herself trying to foresee what
Phyllis's strategy would be. I think I'll take
pains to be rather nice to Mr. Martin. In spite of
his simplicity there's something dangerous about
him. It would be fun to allay his suspicions and
then, when she got him in clear profile against the
sky, shoot him down without mercy. She felt an
agreeable sensation of being on the strong side;
of having underneath her the solid conventions and
technicalities of life—as comfortable and reassur-
ingly supportive as the warm bed itself. Not a
very lucky analogy, perhaps: she looked over at
Ben, who was still asleep on the floor. He looked
pathetic beside the collapsed bed frames, his de-
jected feet protruding at the end of the mattress.
But that was the satisfying thing about Ben: he
was conquered and beaten. He would never surprise her with any wild folly. Urbane, docile, en-
during, he knew his place. Properly wedged into
his seat in the middle of the row, he would never
trample on people's toes to reach the aisle between
the acts. The great fife and drum corps might
racket all around him, he would scarcely hear it.

There was cotton in his ears. Any resolute woman, she reflected sagely, even without children to help her, can drill a man into insensibility.

George allowed the bath water to splash noisily while he cleaned his teeth, but he always turned off the tap while shaving. He shaved by ear as much as by sight or touch. Unless he could hear the crackling stroke of the razor blade he was not satisfied that it was cutting properly.

"How soon do you think the Pony will come?" Janet had asked him as he came upstairs. The children had found some deceptive promotion scheme advertised in a cheap magazine of Nounou's. The notice had led them to believe that if they solved a very transparent puzzle they would easily win the First Prize, a Shetland pony. They had answered the puzzle and now were waiting daily to hear the patter of hoofs up the lane. To George's dismay he had found that they took this very seriously They had swept out an old stall in the stable and ravished a blanket from Rose's bed to keep Prince (whose name and photograph had appeared in the advertisement) from being cold at night. He had tried, gently, to caution them, explaining that the original puzzle had only been preliminary lure for some subscription-getting contest. Undismayed they had badgered Lizzie, the ice man, and a couple of neighbours into sign-ing up at twenty-five cents each. They paid no heed to his temperate warnings that it would be impossible to get many subscriptions for so plebe-ian a journal. He wondered how he would ever be able to disillusion them.

The razor paused and he stared at his half-lathered face in the glass as he realized the nice parallel. Isn't it exactly what Nature is always doing to us? Promising us a Pony! The Pony of wealth, fame, satisfied desire, contentment, if we just sign on the dotted line. . . . Obey that Impulse. By Heaven, what a Promotion Scheme she has, the old jade! Had his sorry dreams been any wiser than those of Janet and Sylvia? His absurd vision of being an artist in living, of know-ing the glamour and passion of some generous fruitful career, of piercing into the stormy darkness that lies beyond the pebbly shallows of to-day— all risible! Life is defeat. Hide, hide the things you know to be true. Fall back into the genial humdrum. Fill yourself with sleep. It's all a Promotion Scheme. . . . And inside these wary counsels something central and unarguable was crying: It wasn't just a Pony. It was the horse with wings.

The great Promotion Scheme, the crude and adorable artifice! How many infatuated subscribers it has lured in, even persuaded them to renew after they had found the magazine rather dull reading. In the course of another million years would it still be the same, man and woman consoling and thwarting one another in their study of the careless hints of Law? He could see the full stream of life, two intervolved and struggling currents endlessly mocking and yearning to one another, hungry and afraid. Clear and lucent in sunlit reaches, troubled and swift over stony stairs, coiled together in dreaming eddies, swinging apart in frills of foam. Sweet immortal current, down and down to the unknown sea. Who has not thrilled to it, craved it, cursed it, invented religions out of it, made it fetich or taboo, seen in its pure crystal the mirror of his own austere or swinish face. Turn from it in horror, or muddy it with heavy feet, this cruel water is troubled by angels and mirrors the blind face of God. Blessings on those who never knew it, children and happy ghosts.

George ran his fingers over his glossy chin. He looked solemn recognition at the queer fellow in the glass, and mused that it's only people who haven't had something they wanted who take the trouble to think confused and beautiful thoughts. But he heard a cautious hand trying the knob. Even thinking about God is no excuse for keeping others out of the bathroom. He laughed aloud, a peal of perfect self-mockery, and splashed hastily into the cold water. Martin, waiting to get in, heard him and wondered. Usually it is only gods or devils who are merry by themselves. Among human beings it takes two to make a laugh.

"Why were you laughing?" he asked, opening his door when he heard George leave the bathroom.

George paid no attention. He was hurrying to tell Phyllis his thoughts before they escaped. Who but she would have endured his absurdities? If she had had hallucinations of her own, that only brought them closer together. Out of these ashes they could rebuild their truth. Love means nothing until you fall into it all over again.

She was sitting on the edge of the bed, by the window, nervously picking the nails of one hand with the forefinger of the other. This habit, which he detested, almost broke his enthusiasm. He had a grotesque desire to tell her that he would forgive her even that. I guess I really do love her enormously, he thought, or the little things she does wouldn't madden me so. Exasperated with sudden tenderness, he had somehow expected her to

meet him with equal affection. But she just sat
there, looking down at her hands. He took them,
to stop the hated gesture. The bantam over the
hill repeated his rollicking sharp salute, which
would have been an epigram if he had uttered it
only once.

"I wish you could stop that rooster," she said.
"Over and over again, the same identical squawk.
I wouldn't mind so much if he wasn't a bantam.
It makes it seem so silly, somehow. He goes out
under those great tall pine trees and shouts at
them."

He smiled and turned her face toward him. She
looked pitiably tired. He knew how she would
look when she was old.

"Perhaps he's rather like me," he said.

"There was one here that crowed just like that
when we were children. The same note exactly."

"It's heredity. Probably this is his great-
great-great-great-grand-egg."

She reached under the pillow, pulled out the
little flattened handkerchief, and stood up.

"I must hurry. I'd give anything if to-day were
over. I suppose life is like this, just day after
day."

"Give me that," he said, taking the handkerchief. "I've seen it before."

"No, you haven't," she said, still in the same dull tone. "It's a new one."

"Yes, I have. Last night."

"Last night?"

"Yes, under your pillow."

"You?"

She stared, her face quivering. Suddenly the line of her mouth seemed to collapse and run downward. Something tight had broken, something proud and fierce had bent. She was crying.

"Oh, Geordie, life is so much queerer than I ever knew. Why didn't you tell me? I had such beastly dreams. I wish I could die."

The old name recalled one of his own for her.

"Leopard, Leopard . . . you silly little half-tamed leopard. What do I care about your dreams? It'll all be all right in the morning."

"It *is* the morning, and it isn't all right. *You* take them for the Picnic, let me stay at home. I *won't* see Mr. Martin. Take him away. He's so like *you*, Geordie, but with all your beastliness left out. Your *nice* beastliness, your *dear* beastliness, everything that makes me hate and adore you."

"Now, listen. I've got a great idea. I didn't half take my bath, I was so keen to tell it to you. Let's get married."

She looked at him in such quaint misery, her

face all wrinkled and slippery with tears, he was almost angry again.

"Damn it, I mean *really* married. The first time doesn't count, it's only a Promotion Scheme, your genial old prayer book admits it. But the Bible says it's better to marry than to burn, doesn't it?"

"Let's do both."

(Why, he thought, she's got almost as much sense as Joyce.)

"That's the way to talk," he said. "Because I'd much rather marry a woman with a sense of humour. All right, we'll pretend we've been living in sin, and now I'm going to make an honest woman of you. Wilt thou, Phyllis, have this man to thy wedded husband——"

"We *have* been living in sin. It's sin to be unhappy and hateful."

"Of course it is. And if either of you know any impediment—— Where's that prayer book of yours? I love that marriage-service stuff so much, it'd be worth while to get spliced every now and then just to hear it. It's so gorgeously earthy. Remember that bit where as soon as he's tied 'em up the parson has misgivings, and sings out in alarm 'O Lord, save thy servant and thy handmaid!'"

"No, don't read me the prayer book now, I can't stand it. I want to get my bath."

"Run along then." He threw her blue robe around her shoulders. "We've got to go through with the Picnic, for the children's sake. We'll make it the happiest day in the world."

"You don't think it's too late?"

He watched her down the passage, and then stood by the window seat looking out. The morning was very moist, there was fog over the bay, the hall had a faint musty odour like damp wallpaper. Certainly it was going to rain. Never mind, it would be one of those steady drumming rains that make a house so cosy. He was surprised to see that Joyce was in the garden already, she had set up her easel near the tea table and was painting. No, he thought, I shan't let her go: we *can* all be happy together. If Phyl knew how much she owes to Joyce she'd fall at her feet. How wise women would be if they knew that a man who has only loved one has never loved any. But better not mention it. Who wants them to be wise, poor . . . half-tamed leopards!

"There's someone in the bathroom," Phyllis said, coming back.

"Martin, probably."

"No, it's Ruth. I can smell her all down the

passage.   That mignonette she uses.   Funny how
sharp one's nose is in damp weather."

"If we ever come here again we'll have the
house repapered."

She knelt on the seat beside him.

"Don't let's come again."

Her look followed his into the quiet garden.
Both were silent.   George guessed well enough
why Joyce was there.   She was doing a sketch for
him, something to leave him.   In that little figure
at the easel was all the honour and disaster of all
the world.

Side by side, his arm about her, he and Phyllis
looked down into the cool green refreshment of
birdsong and dew.   The light was filled with a sense
of mist, too thin to be seen, but sunshine was in-
capable behind it.   Filmy air globed them in, as
the glimmering soap-bubble spheres a breath of
the soap's perfume.   A dream, a fog stained with
dim colour, a bubble of glamour, farce, and despair; all the sane comfortable words are no more
than wind.   One gush of violets rebuts them.
Life is too great for those who live it.   Purposely
they wound and mar it, to bring it to their own
tragic dimension.   What was Joyce's word? . . .
Inadequate.   Yes, not all the beauty of the world

can allay the bitter disproportion. And Time
will come to rob us even of this precious grievance,
this pang we carry in our dusty knapsack like the
marshal's silver baton. And Time will come and
take my lust away. . . .

So learn to live on farce. To savour its venom,
like the Eastern King, dose and larger dose, until
one can relish and thrive on a diet of acid that
would blast the normal heart. Isn't it this very
disproportion that makes the glory? There would
be no laughter in a perfect world. Ever after, di-
gesting his secret poison, he would search other
faces too for the sign of that healing bane.

He felt that Phyllis was about to say something.
He erased his mind, to be ready to receive her
thought; as one parent holds out arms to take the
baby from the other.

"I think she's rather wonderful. I think I
could . . ."

Joy and clean gusto, the blessed hilarity of living! Why, it was so divinely simple, if Phyl
would care to understand. . . .

"Dearest, if you . . . if you only . . ."

The half-tamed leopard stirred and showed a
yellow spark. George's mind, uneasily changing
itself, made swift cusping arcs like the tracks of a

turning car. Ruth came rustling from the bathroom. She was amazed to see them doing a foxtrot together.

"Good-morning!" he said. "Perhaps you didn't know, this is our wedding day."

"Hurry up," he whispered to Phyllis. "Grab the bath while you can. I'll get dressed, I'll just have time to mend that railing before breakfast."

XXI

JOYCE had slipped out early. There was something unbearable in the house's morning stir, its sense of preparation for living in which she would have no part.

Under the pine trees she was far enough from the house to consider it as a whole. She studied its weatherbeaten secrecy. She had the anxious apprehension of the artist, who needs to *feel* his subject, purge it of mere reality, before he can begin work. The long line of the roof sagged a little, like an animal inured to carry burdens. The two semicircled bays, flanking the veranda, kept the garden under scrutiny. Each of all those windows had its own outlook on life. A thread of smoke stole from the kitchen chimney, sifting into the hazy morning. Imperceptible greyness was in the nebulous light, filtered through a gauze of ocean fog. The house was waiting, waiting. That vapoury air dimmed the bright world like breath on a mirror. Yet, for her mood, it was somehow right. A morning of fire and blue would have been indecent.

Houses, built for rest and safety, and then filled with the tension of such trivial sufferings. I wonder if any one has ever done a true portrait of a house? The opaque pearly light now seemed to her more sincere than any glamour of sun or moon. But how reluctant it was to surrender its meaning. She could hear the excited voices of the children, calling to and fro. Her mind was still pursuing something, she didn't know just what. It was like trying to think of a forgotten word. The house hasn't yet quite got over being empty so long, she thought. It's still a little bit empty. Or it believed that being lived in again would be such fun, and now it's disappointed. It had forgotten that life is like this.

She began to paint. This picture was for George, to remind him of things he did not know he knew. It must have love in it, and something more, too. The name of this picture, she said to herself, is A Portrait of a House Saying Good-bye.

The shading was very odd along the veranda, between the two turreted bays and beneath the overhang of the sleeping porch. The light came from no direction, it was latent and diffused, softened in slopes and patches among many angles. She had already dabbed in the profile of the building when she realized what it was that she wanted.

It was not the outside of the house but an interior that was forming in her mind. She left the outline tentative, as it was, and imagined the side of the house to be transparent. Under the sharp projection of the balcony her brush struck through the glassed veranda and found itself in the dining room. The tinted panes gave her a clean spot of colour to focus on. Below these the room was obscure, but then the brush had discovered a pool of candlelight to dip in. Shadowy figures were sitting there, but just as she was about to sketch them they seemed to dissolve from their chairs and run toward the windows, looking outward furtively. There was another, too, outside the little sitting room, whispering in a dapple of black and silver chiaroscuro. Oh, if I could only catch what this means. If someone could help me. If George were here to help me. His large patience, his dear considering voice with the wandering parentheses of thought that she had so often mocked and loved. Voice so near her now and soon so impossible to hear. No one would help her. No one can ever help the artist. Others she saves, herself she cannot save. . . .

She had saved him. She had saved Phyllis's George, given Phyllis the greatest gift of all. Given her back those Georges, enriched with

understanding and fear. But could she save her
own poor phantom, or even herself? At any rate
she was going back to her own life. She thought
of that adored city waiting for her, its steep ge-
ometries of building, its thousand glimpses that
inflame the artist's eye. Extraordinary: you'd
expect to find a painter exultantly at work on
every street corner; and how rarely you see 'em!—
The correct miseries of polite departure, a few
gruesome hours in the train (ripping out the
stitches of her golden fancy) and she would be
there. There, where the whole vast miracle
seemed, in moments of ecstasy, to have been
planned for her special amazement and pleasure.
The subway, with rows of shrewd and weary faces;
girls with their short skirts and vivid scarves; men
with shaven, sharply modelled mouths . . .
the endless beauty of people, and their blessed
insensibility to the infernal pang. . . . Yes,
that was what Phyllis could do for him better
than she: dull and deaden that nerve in his mind:
chloroform George the Fourth, the poor little
bastard!

She was going back to her own life. Back to
the civilized pains of art: its nostalgia for lost
simplicity, its full and generous tolerance, its self-
studious doubt, its divinely useless mirth, its dis-

regard of things not worth discussing among the cheerfully disenchanted. Ah, never try to explain things you know are true. As soon as you begin to do that, they seem doubtful.

A darkness kept coming into the picture. It was as though the silence that had been stored up in that house was now draining out of it, seeping into the absorbent air. The fog was thickening and distorted perspectives. The house was out of drawing. That tricky shadow under the balcony was baffling: it made the whole porch seem out of plumb. Holding up a brush to get a true horizontal, she saw that Martin was coming across the lawn.

"Why, it's Bunny!" he said, pointing to the figure she had suggested with a few hasty strokes. "I know now why she wanted you to help me."

Joyce did not look up.

"You must go, at once," she said.

"I was lying in bed, waiting for it to be time to get up. I saw that some of the wallpaper, by the window, was torn. When I looked at it I found the mouse pattern underneath. It's the old nursery."

"That's what Bunny meant! Go and look in the cupboard, see if you can find it, the mouse I gave you. That's your only chance."

"I think I understand now."

"You mean, you know that we're the same——"

"Yes, that this is what we're all coming to. Except Bunny . . . and—and you. *You* haven't done it, not quite. . . ."

"Martin, I'm worst of all," she cried. "I'm neither one nor the other."

"No, I think Ben is the worst," he said slowly. "It's too bad; he was such a nice boy. Of course George is pretty awful, but I didn't know him before."

"Quick, go away. Don't try to learn too much. You must go for *their* sake. If they find out who you are——"

She had a sick presentiment that they must hurry. And still he lingered, and she could feel Time sloping toward some bottomless plunge.

"Perhaps I don't want to go. There's something I don't quite understand. You all look at each other so queerly: look, and then turn away. And you and George in the garden. What is it? What's happened that hurts you all so?"

How could she answer? How tell him that the world is often too fierce for its poor creatures, overstrains and soils them in their most secret nerves; and that with all their horrors they would not have it otherwise. He had come like the unspoiled essence of living, groping blindly for what

it divines to be happy and real and true; he was
thwarted and damned by the murderous pettiness
of his own scarred brethren. If I had two friends
called Food and Hunger, I'd never introduce them
to each other. Must she, who was born to love
him, be the one to tell him this?

"You *must* go. Don't you see, it isn't only us.
It's you too. You and George. . . . Oh, I
tried not to tell you. George is just you grown up."

He looked at her, appalled.

"You're the George that was once. That's why
he hates you so.—You're George the Fifth, I suppose," she said, forgetting he wouldn't understand.

"I *won't* be like George!" he exclaimed. "But
I shan't go unless you'll come with me. It
wouldn't be any fun unless you were there. Help
us to get away, and we'll never come again."

She did not tell him that she could never go
back; that he must go alone; that they would
always be lonely.

"Are you *sure* ?" he asked pitiably. "Have I
got to be like *that* ? Like George, I mean?"

"Hurry, hurry," was all she could say.

He was running toward the house.

She tried to follow, but some sluggish seizure
was about her limbs. The house, shadowy in

deepening mist, loomed over her. She seemed to hear its passages patter with racing feet. There was a face at the pantry window. Perhaps there was a face at every window. There always is. She dared not look.

There *were* racing feet. The three children burst onto the porch above her.

"Time for breakfast!" they called. "And then we'll be ready for the Picnic!"

Now she knew. The whole dumb face of the house had been warning her; George's premonition last night was the same. She tried wildly to wave them back, but her voice was sealed. Frolicking with anticipation, Janet and Sylvia and Rose ran to the railing and leaned over to shout to her.

"See if there are any cobwebs! If there are, it's not going to rain."

Time swayed over her like an impending tree, tremulous, almost cut through. It seemed so gingerly poised that perhaps the mere fury of her will could hold it stable for a moment. Where was Martin? Oh, if he found the mouse in time he would get back before this happened and perhaps his memory would be wiped clean. She saw George appear at the door of the porch with tools in his hands, and his face turn ghastly.

"We're going to have ginger ale at the Picnic," Sylvia was calling.

She tried to hold Time still with her mind. She was frantically motioning the children back, crying out and wondering whether her voice made any sound. The balustrade was going, she saw the old splintery wood cracking, swaying, sagging. There was a snapping crash of breaking posts. The children's faces, flushed with gaiety, their mouths open, suddenly changed. They leaned forward and still farther forward, holding out their arms to her as though for an embrace. They were beginning to fall. After so many little tears and troubles, how could they know that this was more than one last strange tenderness. And as the railing shattered and they fell, she saw that Martin was at the door of the porch. He had found it.

XXII

THE candles were still smoking on the cake, the children all trooping toward the hall. "Wait, wait!" he cried. "Come back a minute!"

They turned in surprise. The Grown-Ups, very large in the doorway, looked like gigantic prison guards faced by some sudden unexpected insurrection. One of them brushed against the bronze gongs hanging at one side of the door. They jangled softly as if calling them all to attention.

"Don't let's play that game," he said breathlessly. "It's too terrible."

"What game?" asked Mrs. Richmond.

"We made up a game. A game of spies, to——"
He realized that he couldn't possibly explain with the Parents standing there. He caught Joyce's eye. She looked frightened.

"Why, Martin, how silly you are," chirped Phyllis. "Of course we weren't going to play it, not really."

"He's not silly!" Joyce shouted fiercely. "*I* was going to play it."

"So was I," Bunny flashed. "Phyllis is telling fibs. We *were* going to play it. We were going to spy on Grown-Ups, to find out whether they have a good time."

"Bunny, Bunny," said her mother reprovingly. "Tell Phyllis you're sorry. You mustn't forget she's a guest."

"Don't mention it," said Phyllis primly. "When I grow up I'm going to have a lot of children and teach them lovely manners."

"When *I* grow up," Bunny exclaimed, "my children won't never have to say Thank you or they're sorry unless they really mean it."

"When *I* grow up," Ruth said, "I'm going to do without children. They're too much of a burden."

"Perhaps when the time comes," said one of the guards, "they'll find it's not as easy as it sounds."

Martin turned hopelessly to the boys. "Ben, don't *you* grow up. It isn't fun. Ben, I—I *advise* you not to grow up."

"Quit your kidding," Ben retorted. "What's biting you?"

"*Ben!*" exclaimed an indignant parent. "Where on earth do you pick up that way of talking. I'm amazed at you."

Martin saw it was too late. Already something .

had happened. Just the invasion of elders into
the room had changed them all.

"Mother!" he appealed. "Tell the truth, it's
awfully important, cross your heart and hope to
die. *Do* you have a good time?"

A chorus of laughter from the adults.

"Why, dear, what an absurd question. Do we
look so miserable?"

"They won't tell us," he cried bitterly.
"They're all liars!"

There was an appalled silence.

"It's time to get them home. Parties always
upset them. Ben, stop biting your nails."

"Joyce, what on earth are you snivelling about?
Really, it seems as though the more you do for
them the less they appreciate it."

The rain had thinned to a drizzle. Martin
stood uneasily in the hall while the others col-
lected umbrellas and rubbers and repeated their
curtsies. The house smelt of raincoats and fresh
wallpaper.

"Martin, what *is* it? Don't you see I'm busy
talking to Mrs. Clyde? What do you keep twitch-
ing my arm for?"

He had only wanted to ask her if they could
invite Joyce to stay to supper. But he couldn't
shout it out before everyone.

"Well, then, if you didn't want anything special, why are you bothering me? Go and say good-bye to Joyce. Say it politely, and tell her you hope she'll come again. And after that your father wants to speak to you."

But Joyce had already gone, and when she looked back, to try to show him she understood, she did not see him. His father was asking him if a boy ten years old didn't know better than to insult his parents like that.

THE END

CPSIA information can be obtained
at www.ICGtesting.com
Printed in the USA
BVOW03s1139131117
500275BV00001B/35/P